DREAMER

THE FRACTURED FAIRYTALE SERIES

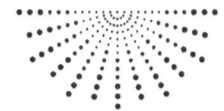

J. A. WYNTERS

Dreamer

Editing by: Emily A. Lawrence

Cover design: The Dust Jacket Designs

Interior Formatting: Dawn Lucous, Yours Truly Book Services

This one is for the ghost.

CHAPTER ONE

Loneliness bites the soul. It is why we are driven to love. And love is tattooed on our very bones, a formula that will either give us peace or destroy us. Love is pain. It is exquisite and chaotic and it despairs, but isn't love meant to hurt? Isn't that how you know it's real?

The silence rumbles through me like thunder; it fills everything inside as I watch her sleep away her life, her youth, my love.

The light breeze carries with it the smell of fresh bread as it drifts from the castle. Here in the underbelly of the town, I can only envision and dream of what it might taste like. The scent plays with my imagination, hot and crisp and fresh, unlike the doughy tough scraps we get. Hunger is a constant friend to me, even better than Tommy, the seamstress' son. He sleeps in the hovel next to mine and always smiles like life hasn't kicked him hard enough yet. I'm jealous. I want to remember what it's like to have my lips stretch so wide and so far and tipped towards the heavens. His mother has taken pity on me. They share their meagre scraps and for whatever reason, she insists on keeping me alive. She promises me a future, but I cannot see beyond the setting of the sun and the constant ache in my bones.

A hum shimmers in the air as the sun rises and dips its rays into hollow cavities, chasing away the chill that has taken over in the night. The town wakes to news of an announcement from the palace and those always carry with them an air of importance. The king and queen say they love all of their townspeople, but I often think they forget about us here in the sewers, the bottom feeders of the land. I do not feel their love. I feel only empty hollowness and despair. But maybe that's the loneliness whispering in my ear, my desire to be cuddled in my damp bed and reassured that it will not always be like this.

People push out of doorways and slink their way to the town square. I follow the flow and push through the gathered crowd. Bodies in rags, skin hanging over walking bones. We are the forgotten, an amassed collection of human scraps. The man who climbs the stage crinkles his nose—our odour must have offended his delicate olfactory senses. But we no longer smell the shit that flows on the street and the rotten fruit discarded by doorways, waiting for the rain to come and wash them away.

He's dressed in palace colours, proud as a peacock with his beautiful feathers and shimmering skin. I smell lavender and oranges and my stomach rumbles. He bathes in fragrances that make my stomach squirm and coil in defeat and hunger.

He clears his throat and pulls a parchment from his belt, his face motionless as he looks over his nose down on us from his perch, awaiting our silence, our obedience, our attention. The murmurs die away and the sun beats down on us with its heavy harsh cane. Sweat licks its way down my cheek and I stick out my tongue, catching the salty dew. It tastes worse than yesterday.

The man unrolls the parchment and a broad smile slashes his face. "The king and queen wish to announce that they are expecting a baby girl. On the day of her birth, they will hold a grand celebration to mark the occasion and the castle gates will open. You shall all dine and lavish your best wishes onto our monarchs."

The crowd erupts in cheers around me. I don't know if they are happy for the baby or for the food. All I know is that in this moment I hate that child, for it's going to be born into love, into comfort. She will always have all of her heart's desires and the more she has, the less I will.

The man, having read the parchment and delivered his news, descends the platform and reaches for his horse. A huge beast. Neighing at the touch, it shakes its head and a frenzy of shiny long black hair shivers along its neck. White froth foams and bubbles at his mouth. My stomach twists. I could feed off him for months.

Two palace guards wing the horse and wait for their master to ascend the animal. Clad in heavy armour and holding long, menacing spears, only their eyes shine from behind their helmets. When he gives the signal, the guards order the crowd to make way, and like an old rag, they pull apart like fabric ripping at the seams. The visitors trot away to cheers and all I can think about is the burning inside me. The heated hate I feel for this child who will never be like me.

Hate is like smoke. It is uncontainable. It spreads and filters into everything and colours the insides black. I carried my hate for five long months. Each day, amid the heat or the rains, the churning of my empty stomach or the waking from my restless sleep. It grew heavy, like the belly of the queen and like her, I wanted to expel it from my body.

They say that on the night the princess was born, the crescent moon shone through the queen's window and kissed her newly flushed cheeks. I remember that it laughed at me instead. The moon didn't have kisses for sewer rats, only disdain.

But I don't care, for the baby was born and I would free myself too in the morning.

When the sun rises, the streets swarm with men and women. Torn rags have been patched and flowers replaced the dirt and rot usually reserved for us. Faces are clean and hands are washed, and the air feels sickly and sweet. The people seem spellbound, mesmerized by the promise of food. But I have other ideas.

As instructed, I wash my face and wring out the dirt from my shirt, which dries on my body as we walk to the castle. I carry with me a heavy secret and a small knife I have crafted with my own hands. It's crude and blunt, but death doesn't have to be swift or beautiful. It can be slow and agonising— like starvation.

Determination steels my features as we approach the castle gates. In all my years, they have never been opened. As I cross the threshold, anger slices whatever doubts I may have had about my plans. The pain searing my chest as if my own weapon has sliced itself into my ribs.

Beyond the walls that kept us outside lies lush, splendid lawns, green so crisp I fear the blades would shatter beneath my feet. The wealth emanates from the ground itself and I notice the agitation of the crowd I had follow. They feel an unease, for we do not belong. Yet as we swarm deeper into the castle walls, we are swallowed whole by humanity, so much so, that it no longer matters who is royal and who is not. People came from far and wide, invitations spread across the entire country. Such is the stretch of our land.

I have no concept of its size nor cultures nor people, but of two things I am certain. Despite the vastness and wealth, we—down in the sewers—have somehow managed to remain hidden and forgotten, and no matter where you come from people like food.

It's clear to me that the place in which I live is full of abundance, and thus, I can't understand why the men and women before me are rounded and pudgy and pink-cheeked, while my bones carry my skin about like a chore.

Music and laughter fill the air and snatches of merry conversations swim around me like lost glistening fish, but it's the smell that has my body quaking and needing. It wants to feast like the others. Tables covered in crisp yellow cloth are laden with more food than I've ever seen. Meat and fruit and mead spill on the table as greedy hands snatch at the sticky delights. My body screams for nourishment, it aches for it and yet, their fanciful gifts cannot deter me from my task.

The afternoon drags and the sun stretches lazily across the perfect blue sky. It seems even the sun itself has come to greet this princess, this girl who will keep taking everything from me. My jaw clenches and I grind my teeth. Three have fallen in the back, yet to be replaced. I wonder if new ones will sprout in their place. My body wars with my mind, hunger and hatred in a ring around a rosy. I wonder which will fall first.

When the trumpets sound across the court, the crowd cheers. A wild cry and full of jubilation, while my bitter heart chugs in my throat. My hatred so raw and vile it wants to spill from me.

The king and queen call the people forward and they huddle into the court, each pushing and shoving, tipping against one another in a mad wave to get a glimpse of the newborn girl. It's here that starvation works in my favour. My lithe form and agile legs propel me forward as I push my way through the undulating crowd. When the bodies become too thick to advance, I fall to my hands and knees and crawl at their feet, just as I have always done. Gipping my weapon in my hand, I see the raised stage ahead of me. Intricate stonework that only a master stonemason could have accomplished.

I pull myself from the floor, my patched-up rags dishevelled and stained. I grip the handle of my weapon and suck a long stream of air into my lungs, knowing it may be my very last, then glance up at the stage to find my target.

When my gaze lands upon her face, I stand frozen, mesmerized, for she is indeed the most beautiful thing I have ever seen in all of my short life. Nestled in her mother's arms and wrapped in a white cotton blanket that cocoons her and shelters her from the world, I no longer want to harm her, but protect her. The weapon falls from my hands as I gaze upon the sleeping child, wanting nothing more in this world than to have my arms wrapped around her and assure her that no harm would ever come to her, that she will be loved and cherished. Always.

But even as I lovingly gaze upon her face, thunder rumbles above us and a flash of lightning branches across the sky. The crowd shudders for a moment before a deathly silence falls upon them and they part like a deer being butchered and cleaved in half.

The king struggles to rise under the eerie stillness that has captured the crowd. When he at last stands to his full height, he looks upon the new guest who has so divided his guests.

"Good evening, your majesty," she croons.

"Good evening." The king's voice shudders and with it my heart.

The old woman creeps slowly along the path that was created for her. Dressed entirely in black, she's slightly hunched over and her long white hair stands about her like a wild mane framing her gnarled face. She makes her way to the baby and holds out her hands to the queen. The queen's lips stretch in an agonised smile as she hands her baby over to the woman.

My heart clinches in my chest and my fingers search for the weapon I have dropped. Scanning the floor, I cannot find it and my small fists squeeze the emptiness. I chastise myself for my foolishness, for how could I ever protect my princess without a weapon. I'm nought but a weak boy. Anger and self-loathing seed themselves in my belly where food should have been instead. I feel the fool that I was disallowing myself to feast, as my gaze returns to the stage, where the old hag is hugging the baby to her chest, a tiny yellow curl bouncing on her forehead.

The woman turns to her parents in disgust. "And why was I not worthy of an invitation to celebrate the birth of such a treasure?"

The dismayed king and queen can do nothing but mumble a pathetic apology. The old woman cackles at their empty excuses and turns to the baby in her arms.

"Such an innocent little thing, isn't she?" She rocks the baby against her chest. The queen lets out a soft whimper and my heart lurches in my chest as if it wants to shoot out.

My body shakes like a leaf, helpless in the wind, and so too I stand helpless. "Would be a pity if she grew up in such a cruel, cold world where everyone is judged on their wealth and beauty instead of their qualities."

At this the king takes courage. "And what qualities do you possess?"

"A fair share more than some of your other guests."

As one the crowd follows her gaze, which falls on his daughter's three godmothers. Three fair maidens with lovely faces and desirable features, the pampered daughters of noblemen who travelled lavishly. The women take a step back in unison and when I look back, the old lady smiles at them knowingly.

"What are you talking about? They have brought our daughter gifts and will watch over her till her wedding day." The king chokes on his own words, his face peppered with sweat as if he's running a fever, his eyes slack, glued onto his daughter. His legs stiff, forced to remain in place.

"She has already been promised?" The woman's head tilts slightly, a tired eyebrow raised.

The kind offers a curt nod as if he's not ready to have shared the news.

Promised? The word strikes a match inside me, though I'm not entirely sure why.

"Indeed." The old pedlar woman nods before smiling a crooked smile at the baby in her arms and laying a kiss on her forehead. The baby girl coos and wiggles, and her eyes open for the first time that day.

They are not as I expected. They are the colour of the sky, but not blue like on a summer's day but grey, and stormy, like already her head is full of thoughts and ideas that form storms inside of her.

"And who might be the lucky man?"

The king clears his throat. "Prince Aamon."

The woman's face falls into a scowl, the lines on her face deepening in long, deep crevices.

The queen, having held her husband's hand the entire time, lets out a soft squeak. Her body sways as if she wants to step forward but is locked in place. "Thank you for your visit with our Dolores. Can I have my baby back?"

At the sound of her name, I know it to be etched on my very bones. They rattle with the sound of it, and I know that that name will forever hold power over me. As beautiful and delicate as the baby herself.

"In a moment." The old woman's words sound like a warning set into place by the thunder clapping above us. "I have brought the princess a gift," she shouts over the crowd, who like a tree battered by fierce winds leans backwards, as if afraid.

All but me, for I lean in, eager to know what this gift might be, while feeling inadequate at being unable to shower the baby with gifts, for I already know she deserves the world. I cannot believe that just a few moments ago she was my mortal enemy. I swallow the shame of my foolishness.

The old woman looks at the king and queen. "You have sealed her fate and cursed this child." She turns to the baby in her arms, her voice rising, her words quickening. "I will save you from the ill fate your parents assigned you to. For on your eighteenth birthday, you will fall into a deep slumber where you will only be awakened by the man who loves you most. When his lips touch yours, he will return you to this world and you will know all the truths." Her words are sealed with a flash of lightning that cleaves the sky.

"No!" The king lunges at the woman, but it's too late, for her spell was cast and the princess was doomed.

The old woman slides aside and away from the king's arms, setting a light kiss on the baby's head. She places her back in her crib and makes her way off the stage, her face twisting with each step as if walking is agonising. I hope it is, for she has just cursed the baby I have sworn to protect. Already I have failed. I glare at the old lady, my long, dirty nails digging into my palms as fury slithers inside me, deadly and vicious, and yet as she walks by me I can do nothing but scowl.

She stops before me and her face softens as my body stands frozen, unable to unleash the wrath bubbling inside it.

"You cursed her." I manage. My voice small and childish in the large space.

She smiles and reaches out to me, but even as I try to flinch away, her long finger has already swiped away the tears I didn't know slid down my cheeks. "I saved her, boy, and one day you will too."

Confusion and anger clog my throat and no more words will come. The woman creeps away till she clears the palace walls, a lightning strike sealing her departure.

The air splits with Dolores' shrill cries and they awake the mass. The queen runs to the crib and lifts her crying baby into her arms. I watch in fascination how her blotched face crinkles and tears run down her reddening skin. Her tiny arms grasping at the air, searching for comfort. I want to run to her then and envelope her in my arms and promise her I will make everything ok, keep all her pain away, forever. Her tiny lips quiver and her cries go on, broken only by her gasping for breaths in between. But even as I try to run toward the stage, the crowd behind me erupts into a mad swarm. Limbs and bodies scurry away screaming, tossing me about as they run.

The gallop sounds like thunder as a herd of mounted horses bursts from the stables, each carrying an armoured man. The chestnut beasts, already sweating, whine as they fly out of the gates. They swarm out of the palace, hooves meeting the earth below them in full valour, as they mow down anyone still in their path to capture the wench.

When the sound of hooves is nothing more but echoes

and the tables overturned with spilled food and sobs pierced the air as women hover over the dead and wounded, I only have eyes for her. My ears burn only with her relentless cries that slash at my heart, a piercing sound that torments my very soul. It's probably the reason I don't see him as my legs carry me towards her, and my arms crave to feel her soft baby flesh and shelter her from the world.

The thundering of hooves should have warned me, but I can only hear her calls. The lone stallion gallops through the gates, a straggler. His inky mane wisped in the air like black flames. He's a beast, a demon whose muscles ripple from under his freshly groomed pelt. His powerful legs propel him forward, driven on by the soldier mounted atop his back. The pain is brief and sharp as the beast rides over me like an invisible obstacle. I roll beneath its feet, sucked in by the power, and tumble into the ground. The last sound as starburst erupts behind my eyes is his hoof as it knocks against my skull.

CHAPTER TWO

My eyes rip open and pain invades my head like a foreign and devastating army. They fall closed again, trying to shut out the sharp throb that slices along my face. I feel like I should cry, but I don't. Crying would hurt more. I clench my teeth, trying to keep the pain from spilling to the rest of me, but I fail. Breathing felt like a burden. It would be easier to stop. But I can't, just like I can't stop the whimper that slides out of my mouth.

"Shhh, boy, it's ok."

The voice is warm and soft but unrecognisable. My eyes snap open and pain mingles with fear and dips in confusion.

Time trickles. My gaze roams the strange room and details seeped into my head, which throbs and wants to remain empty and white, like the soft blanket *she* was wrapped in. The brief thought allows me a second of comfort.

The woman who hovers about me is large, larger and rounder than any who live in the lower parts of the kingdom. Her pudgy cheeks are tinted with red and her kind eyes are sunken into her rounded face. Her hair is streaked in white and forehead creased in a myriad of crevasses that resemble the cracked earth when it stops raining.

"You've taken a nasty knock to the head." She speaks softly as if she knows sound amplifies my pain. To her left is a bowl, large and bronzed and unlike any I've seen before. She dips a cloth into it and wrings it out. The water ripples and shimmers over the surface.

Candles flicker around us, drab walls, cool, like in a cave. I feel trapped. I want to scream but only a pathetic sound slips out.

"Shhh, boy." Her damp cloth sears my face and pain explodes behind my eyes. "Rest now, it will be ok."

When I wake again, the room remains the colour of wet dirt, drab and reddish and shimmering in the flickering candlelight. The woman has moved away, but the pain remains. She stands by the other side of the room and looks to be slicing bread. The smell twists my empty stomach, and a moan slips from between my lips. The woman turns. Her smile is swallowed in her pudgy cheeks and yet somehow it is lovely.

"You're awake again, boy."

I nod as she states the obvious, the movement shooting a thrill of pain across my face and body.

"You took a right blow. You're lucky that horse didn't kill you."

Am I? Am I lucky?

"No one claimed you after you fell."

Why would they? There's no one left to claim me. I belong to no one, only to myself. And to her.

"You must be hungry." She shuffles over with a wooden plate and places it on the table. Three thick slices of bread and a red gelatinous goo sit on the plate. My stomach churns and aches. "Come, eat, it's fresh. It will help you heal."

My eyes lock onto the food and my belly screams, yet all I can do is breathe. Even though it hurts, I inhale slow, deep breaths, waiting for the pain to wane. Hunger nudges at me, poking me from the inside, urging me on, forcing my movements till I sit up. Sharp pain lances through my head and stars collide behind my eyes. Nausea climbs up my throat, but I don't worry. There is nothing inside me to bring up.

I slide off the bed to find myself in nothing but my undergarments, my bare body flecked in darkening welts, my skin lumpy where it should be smooth. My head spins as I stand up and stagger towards the table. With each step, I feel daggers in my abdomen—my limbs heavy, uncooperative.

I fall into the wooden chair and want to scream, but my mouth is clogged with saliva and my throat seals with emotion.

"Eat," she says and nudges the plate towards me.

I slide my finger into the red goo. It's cool and wobbly with tiny seeds swimming inside it.

"It's jam, boy, have you never had jam?"

Jam. I shake my head and this time her smile is sad. I know because it looks the same as when they came to tell me my parents were dead and I'll be ok. They patted my shoulder and smiled. Like that.

"Dip your bread in it and eat."

I do as she says. The jam coats my tongue, and it is like nothing I have ever tasted. An explosion of sweet delight glazes my mouth like I have bitten sunshine. The tiny seeds dance on my tongue before sliding into my stomach, which accepts them with delight. Jam is my favourite thing in this world.

Yet despite the wonder of jam, I wince at the pain each time I bend or flex, stretching against the will of my joints. Eating is splendid torture.

The plate sits empty between us and my stomach growls. It's angry now, unsure what to do with so much inside. It protests and fights, pushing the invading food out. I grit my teeth and swallow. I don't know when I'll eat again. I don't know if I'll ever have jam.

"You ate that quickly. You were hungry, weren't you?"

I nod. If I speak, I might return her meal.

"You don't say much, do you?"

I shrug, scared to open my mouth.

She sighs and gives me another sad smile. "Get some rest, boy, we'll decide what to do with you in the morning."

I drag my body back to the bed and collapse onto the mattress. Cold sweat erupts across my forehead as the pain swims just beneath my skin. It throbs and burns and plays havoc with my brain till I concede to the torment and the darkness.

This is my first lesson in real pain. It drags on like a wounded animal and I know now it will be a companion, at least for a while, until I heal.

The light hasn't changed. Flickering candles, yellows and reds. Time doesn't exist here, just pain and jam.

I like the jam.

The woman sits and watches me. Her face shifts when she realises I am awake. I can't tell if the shift is good or bad yet. I can't tell if it's morning. My only two certainties are pain and hunger.

"Are you hungry, boy?"

I nod.

She grunts as her chair squeals against the floor, and she shifts her large body to the back of the room. She comes back with more bread and more jam. It's somehow easier to navigate through the pain as I make my way to the table.

Indulgence is a dangerous chasm and yet I have fallen into it so quickly. While the jam entices my body, my mind wanders. How much jam could I consume to look like her?

"Do you have parents, boy?"

I shake my head, my mouth stuffed with flaky fresh bread. It melts in my mouth and I shove another piece as soon as the first disappears.

"Do you know where you are?"

I shake my head again, no longer looking at her pudgy face, shovelling the food into my mouth, unable to savour.

"You're in the palace."

My hand freezes midway to my mouth like it's been caught in a spider's web. It dangles and tosses through the air and my gaze finds hers.

"Do not be afraid," she says and yet my heart feels like it might rupture. It gallops like the chestnut herd that chased the old crone. There is no stopping its force. But it is not fear that possesses it so, but sheer joy, for I share a roof with *her*. The thought brings me strength and, reaching for the bread once more, I tear off a generous piece and stuff it into my mouth.

The woman nods in approval, her eyes softening in their fatty casings. "Would you like to stay?"

I stop eating once again and my head tilts a little. Suspicion crawls inside me like maggots. I scan the scant room, the bare walls and two mattresses pushed against opposite walls, the tiny dining room table with two chairs. Two plates, two sets of cutlery. My eyes land back on the woman whose pensive face seems lost as she looks at my face.

"There were two of us once." Is all she gives in explanation. "You'll be safe and warm and I have plenty of jam."

My eyes dart to the red blob on my plate and back to the woman's face. "You can call me Agatha," she says. "If you want to stay."

It's a statement that sounds like a question. And many of

my own trickle through my head. But it's as if she could see them. "You'll stay here in the palace with me. You'll have to work, same as everyone, but we'll have each other."

I think of my damp bed and the seamstress who sometimes gave me scraps of food with no jam. I think of the hunger that's plagued me endlessly like a sickness. I think of the darkness that hugs me instead of my mother, how it hisses in my ear till I shake with tears. But mostly I think of *her*. I could watch over her from here. I can protect my princess and love her.

I nod and Agatha's face explodes in a smile that makes her cheeks quiver and her eyes sparkle. I see what I am for her, a replacement. But I don't care. She has jam.

CHAPTER THREE

Sunlight splinters across my eyes and I squeeze them shut before they open again slowly against the bright light. My bruises have turned yellow and though it's still a little hard to breathe, my body is healing.

Agatha has fashioned a hat to cover my wounds. The damaged skin scarred and crackled like a dried riverbed over my face. She says it's not appropriate to meet the king with such ugliness. It's why she also insisted I wash. A large bucket with warm water that smells of jasmine and cloves. I still don't understand why they wash themselves in food. I liked the warmth. It's new. There are so many new things here.

Nothing here is like it is where I was before. Everything is clean and screams of abundance. I remember it's the reason why I hated the princess, but now as I draw ever closer to the hall, my body feels as if it's composed entirely of butterflies and any minute they will all take flight and flutter away.

The courtyard looks different now. The hanging flowers, long now gone, no doubt dishevelled and dead, the tables of food packed away, no music or laughter, just a strange murmur, an undercurrent of something other than joy. But these things don't matter to me, for I am but a few steps away from the hall where last I saw my princess.

The stone building is magnificent, towering over the land. It is the biggest thing I have ever seen and the shadow it casts looms over the sewers in the afternoons and steals the sun. A few people mill about, conversations and discussions. They wear serious faces and long frowns. Surrounding the walls are stationed the king's guards in their shiny armour and closed helmets. Their presence meant to spell safety and fear.

"Agatha." The king smiles down at the woman who's taken me as her own, his face breaking into a warm smile. She immediately drops to one knee, head bowed. When I do not follow, she snatches my hand and pulls me to the ground.

"Your majesty." Her lips tremble, spurring the dark hair on her upper lip in a wild dance.

"Get up, get up."

Sour disappointment bubbles in my throat as I keep searching the room. The princess is not here. My pathetic heart feels as though it is shrinking inside my chest, which tightens and hurts as though it needs to recede too to accommodate for my disappearing heart. I am no longer listening to Agatha and the king, though wisps of conversation wriggle themselves through me, 'the boy, the witch, to be kept, to be trained, mine.'

A sudden hush falls on the room and once again I am pulled to the floor, but this time when I look up, there she is, in her mother's arms. I can't help but be drawn to her face, the tiny creature in her mother's arms no bigger than a sac of sugar from the market. A few tiny ties peek from the blanket, and a single curl rests on her angelic face. I'm taken aback once again by her, her beauty, her vulnerability. I'm filled with awe. As if she feels my eyes on hers, they snap open and her wailing begins, a sad screeching lament of want.

The king squeezes his wife's hand and they both fawn

over the crying baby. Anger bubbles inside me. They should be doing something, not smiling at her. She's in pain. Before I can think about it, I rush to the stage. She needs me. I'm her protector.

Two gleaming spears halt my advance. Two guards seal my path. Their large bodies tower over me, shielding her from me. There is a new kind of sound. A stunned silence pierced by severe wails that sting my heart.

"Let him pass." It's the king's voice and the silence feels heavier still.

The guards step away and my gaze falls on the crying baby. Her puffed cheeks reddening with effort, her tiny face creased, sliced with tears.

I take a cautious step. My eyes flit to the king.

"What are you doing, boy?"

Fear slithers around my throat and chokes me. A grunt leaks out as I desperately look at the princess, her wails tearing at my soul.

"You're worried about Dolores?"

Dolores. The name glides through me and coats my bones, cementing around them. Her name resonates inside me like a tolling bell. Its lament is beautiful and endless. I want to weep.

"She's fine..." He assures me while his gaze turns to his wife. She gives him a slight nod, reaffirming. "Just a little heartburn."

Heartburn? Is it set on fire just like mine?

"Would you like to hold her?" The queen takes a small step towards me and her husband snaps his head towards her. She ignores him as she steps closer.

I nod. I would. I want to wrap myself around her and show her how this world could feel safe.

"Sit." The queen's tired face softens as she smiles gently at me. I do as she says. My heart quakes in my chest and my very bones threaten to shift. She detaches the wailing baby from her chest and places her into my arms. She fits into my arms like a seed into the soil, taking root around my heart. I cradle her and she wriggles as I draw her closer still. I want to feel her heart burn against mine.

Her head nuzzles against my chest and her tears dry. I want to drink this moment in, this moment with my princess in my arms. Her grey eyes are more brilliant than I remembered, and they study mine, curious and young. Everything is still a mystery to her. She has so much to be fascinated by. The flame of my heart brightens as I'm currently the object of that fascination.

I don't notice the silence, not while I smile down at the baby, now cooing, her tiny lips pressed together, her large eyes learning, taking everything in, every detail, every part of my face. It's intrusive and exhilarating all at once.

"She stopped crying," the queen whispers, shattering the silence.

A low murmur picks up around the room and for the first time I sense every pair of eyes on me. They've also been studying me.

The baby—now content—closes her eyes. Her face nestles against my chest and her hot breath cuts through the thin fabric of my new shirt and heats my skin. I'm paralysed with fear and awe.

"She likes you," the queen says and gifts me a radiating smile. I tip my head and decide that I'll save all of mine for her daughter, but my heart stalls at her words. She likes me— and I love her.

"He's a scrawny little thing." The king moves his attention back to Agatha, who's been standing open-mouthed and silent, gaping at me.

"Yes, your majesty," she stutters her answer and rips her eyes away from me.

"And you want to keep him?"

"Yes, your majesty."

I feel his gaze shift to mine and I meet his thoughtful eyes. There is a deep-seated kindness and warmth that lies in the deep blue and I wonder where that kindness hides when it comes to the forgotten in the sewers.

"He'll have to work."

"I can use another pair of hands down in the kitchen."

The king's long fingers slide into his beard. They look like white worms wiggling in mud. "He won't replace your Damian."

Her round face drops, all the joy collapsing away, and her gaze finds the floor. She nods, a small movement that seems as though it's taken the last of her energy.

"You may go." The king dismisses her.

"Come on, boy," she calls me. My gaze drifts away from the sleeping baby and finds her shimmering eyes, then the queen's, who holds out her hands, wanting to rip my heart from my chest. I look at the baby's face, stealing a final glance, burning her perfect image into my being. She's already a part of me.

I'm loath to release her and as soon as she is out of my grasp I feel the sinking black emptiness. A vast, endless void that will follow me like a shadow till I get to hold her again.

I shuffle behind Agatha. She swaggers, a hop to her step. She's happy while my heart remains in this hall, pulling farther and farther away.

"Hurry up, boy." She's yelling again and I wipe the sweat that leaks from my hairline. "The prince will be here soon."

The prince. An invisible enemy I hate. My princess has been promised to him. We've spent the better part of the morning baking. Bread and cakes and pastries he will get to enjoy while he sits in her company and I watch from the shadows.

The hate seeps into my work, my pastries refusing to rise, remaining flat like my spirits, coming out of the oven black and charred like my insides. Agatha fumes. She's hot and angry like the furnace, but far more forgiving.

The whispers have already started. Murmurs of an elegant carriage pulled by six horses all wearing plumage. The arrival of another royal family from afar. A charming king and queen and their fair son. My body itches to leave, to lurk. I want to see this boy, the boy who has stolen her from me before she was ever mine.

A frustrated Agatha sends me away. "You're more trouble than you're worth today," she hollers and waves me off, but I know that later when I return to our room, she will give me an extra slice of bread in way of apology.

We have grown accustomed to one another. Her love is gentle and fierce like a low flame that always burns. It's warm and inviting and rarely bites. I give her back what I can, but my heart burns only for Dolores.

I hide in the long shadows and watch them as they ascend the carriage, their bodies bathed to the knees in sunset after a day's long journey. The guards escort them into the hall where a set table awaits.

The king and queen sit at the head of the table, and next to them a tiny crib holding a sleeping Dolores. She's so peaceful, her face is a salve to the fierce anger that's stewed inside me all day. Across from them sit their guests, a man and a woman with milky skins and dark hair, they wear smiles like masks. Besides them sits the boy, my nemesis, the one who makes my burning heart feel charred and ashen. He is fair-haired and well-mannered. He smiles and coos at Dolores. His clothes are tailored and fine, and he converses with confidence, even for a boy who seems to be no older than I am.

He's perfect. I draw in a long breath that fans the flame of my heart. Dolores deserves perfect and he can give her everything a princess like her deserves.

I remain watching them, stealing glances at the sleeping baby. I can see our futures in this room. She will sit beside her new husband tucked between two sets of parents and they will all exchange smiles and conversation and eat, while I watch her from the shadows.

The thought fills me with content. I will watch her, *over* her, forever.

The morning air is crisp and winter will soon set its claws into the land, blanketing it with white and cold. My mind wanders to Tommy, the seamstress' son. I wonder if he will survive it. Guilt pinches my gut as I discard the thought like the dirty water in my bucket. Movement catches my eye and I swivel to glimpse a wisp of fair hair.

I set the bucket down and steal along the walls till I spot the prince. He walks briskly, checking over his shoulder every few paces. He stays to the shadows, just like me, and makes his way to the kennels where the king's prized bitch birthed four brown puppies. They are soft like the princesses' hair and brown like the earth after the rain.

I've watched them run around and nip at one another playfully. The smaller of the four lets me pat its head and licks my hand while wagging his tiny tail. His liquid dark eyes are full of expression and emotion and a part of me loves him. Agatha keeps telling me to give it a name, but I haven't been able to think of anything that suits.

The prince opens the door to the kennels and kneels down. I know the mother is out on her morning walk with the groomer. The four puppies run to him eagerly. He holds out his hand and pats their heads and for a long moment I watch this boy take away one more of the things that never belonged to me and give it the love that I can't. But before I tear my eyes away and leave, the prince pulls his hand away and screams at the puppies. "You bit me!"

They cower for a second before continuing to jump and wiggle their tails. The prince smiles at the puppy and pets it again, scratching behind his ears as he does. The puppy's tail wags like a mad pendulum.

"Good boy." The prince brushes his hand along the brown fur. "You're just a puppy, aren't you?" He lifts the dog onto his lap as something dark settles across his face. "But that's no excuse." He grabs the puppy by the scruff of the neck, then viciously hurls him into the wall. The yelp is shrill and agonised. The dazed puppy whimpers as it stands, one of his tiny feet elevated.

"Oh, I'm so sorry, boy." The prince's voice has softened with his expression. "Are you hurt, little one?" He pats his knees and the puppy's eyes light up before his tail remembers its rhythm and he hobbles over to the prince. "You really are a stupid beast."

It's then the prince stands up and cocks his leg before kicking the puppy with full force. The dog yelps as he flies through the air, the sound deadening as he hits the back wall, his little head thudding against the bricks.

My heart stops with his.

His act, a betrayal of love itself, an abandonment of goodness, and for the first time I see the transient monster that resides behind his fair hair and blue eyes, the real evil that lurks inside him and the witch's words vibrate inside me.

'I saved her, boy, and one day you will too.'

The puppies gather around their breathless brother. He lies like a lump of clay, frozen forever in time. They yelp and nip at him, but his lifeless body remains limp at their feet. The whimpers leek from the kennel like a sad song and red stains the prince's cheeks as he begins to yell.

"Shut up, you stupid mutts. He bit me!" He picks up a second pup. It yaps as he grabs him by the collar and shakes him, but before he can do anything else, howling sounds in the distance. The prince swivels and looks about, his eyes roaming the laneway.

He throws the pup down. It skids along the straw and yelps unhappily. "Lucky your mother is coming back," the prince hisses at the remaining litter, then steps out of the kennel, closing the door behind him. He looks about once more before walking casually back towards the castle. I sink into the shadows as he walks by me, a smirk decorating his face like a twisted trophy.

CHAPTER FOUR

Five years later

"Come look," Dolores calls me and I chase after the little girl. She giggles and sinks into the green sea. The weeds wave around her and she calls me again. "Quick."

I fall in beside her and catch a glimpse of the lizard before it scampers off the rock and disappears behind the long grass.

"Awe! You scared him!" Her little face scrunches up and her mouth turns down.

I huff out a laugh and she scowls at me, her grey eyes marbled and shiny.

I fall onto my back and tuck my hands behind my head, closing my eyes and letting the sun stroke my face. These rare afternoons with Dolores are my favourites. Agatha dismisses me from the kitchen when our work is done, and the queen surrenders to the nagging of her five-year-old daughter to let her run around with the boy.

She looks to me like a big brother, a protector, a playmate. I often bring her to the meadows. We like it here. The stillness of the world. Where there are no duties or hierarchies or chores or brushed hair or fancy dresses. But mud and grass and critters to chase.

Sometimes we bring a ball and play. But my favourite is when we lie down together with her head on my chest and look up at the sky and let the sun kiss our faces and I can hear her breathe.

Most of the time she complains, and I let her ramble on. I love the sound of her sweet voice. She complains about having to learn etiquette and wearing tight dresses and wonders why she has to sit with the king and queen for dinner and eat all her food and why she can't see me more often and how she has no other friends to play with.

Her problems belong to a five-year-old princess. I've never complained about having to eat all my food. But I don't mind, because her insignificant problems are colossal to her and she only shares them with me. Secrets that she unburdens in whispers and whines.

"Next time be more careful," she scolds me and comes to lie by my side. Her wild, long blond hair falls around her delicate face and she smiles up at me encouragingly.

I nod at her and her mouth stretches in a beautiful smile. I am forgiven.

"Did you know Mother wants me to try on a new dress?"

I shake my head and prepare myself for another session of endless, pointless complaints. I can rest while she speaks and enjoy the melody of her voice.

"For when the prince comes."

At that my eyes fly open and my heart contracts and expands all at once. I sit up and look at her smiling face, contentment and excitement laced across her features.

"Mother said I've been promised to him. She said he is very sweet, like you." She smiles at me and my heart cracks beneath it.

"Have you met him? Mother said he's visited once before." She doesn't let me answer. Her words keep tumbling out of her mouth. "I wonder if he'll come to play with us. Do you think we could all be friends?"

Once when I was helping Agatha set the royal table for lunch, I dropped one of the plates. It was perfectly white with a gold rim, and when it shattered, the pieces were still beautiful, and if I was to put them back together the plate would still be usable, but it would never be perfect, it would be cracked and parts of it would always be missing. Dolores reminds me of that plate, her perfectly milky skin and golden hair. If she knew the truth, it would break her. I didn't want to break another beautiful thing. Not when it was Dolores.

Her melodic voice falls away as a long shadow looms over us. The guard that follows us around everywhere and watches our every move has come to cut our time short. Again. My disdain for him grows each time I see Dolores. His impatience stabs at me.

Dolores stands timidly and reaches for my hand. Her lithe fingers lace with mine and I lead her back to the castle. We're silent, but her excitement moves through her like a current that burns my skin.

At the gates, she pulls her hand away and calls me. I fall to my knees and she wraps her tiny hands around me "I love you," she whispers in my ear and for a few brief moments my worries fall away and my heart burns. She nuzzles her little head into my neck, her hair perfumed with flowers and earth.

She releases me and I allow it, before she gifts me with a beautiful smile. The guard leads her away. She bounces and bounds as if the gravel beneath her feet is nothing but air.

My heart dips like an anchor.

The shredded meat drips and saturates the bread, the smell making my mouth water as Agatha shoves it in my face. "Eat." She scowls at me.

I grab the food and stuff it into my mouth.

"What's gotten into you today?" She's angry again and I can't blame her. "Look at the mess you've made!"

My body has been a growing den of vipers all day, snapping and slithering inside me. Anxiety grips me and my appetite drips away mid chew. Memories of the prince's cold eyes and entitled smirk haunt me as his carriage approaches the castle.

I force the food down, not wasting a single drop. I know my princess will need a protector and I can't be that when I'm weak. Agatha has kept me well fed. My body grows stronger every day.

I put away my dish and Agatha nods in approval.

"Go now, I have more work to do."

I slink away from the kitchen and gather myself into the little shadowed nook at the base of the hall. I have spent many nights here watching over my princess as she plays with her food and sings to her mother, as she cries over chaffed knees and recalls her day.

But today I am here to watch over her, for the enemy draws near.

The table has been set in much the same way as it was during his previous visit, except that a chair replaces the crib. I'm relieved to see it's set across from the others.

My body cramps as I wait. The trumpets sound across the yard and voices slide beneath the heavy wooden door of the hall. The enemy has arrived and is shown to his chambers to rest and freshen up before he meets my Dolores. I watch the shadows grow and stretch across the floor like a waking beast.

The small group arrives and takes their seats. My princess

smiles at the prince and he in turn smiles back. He has grown. He is at least one head taller than he was and his shoulders have grown broader, his face longer, and his hair lighter still, like strings of bleached yellow light.

The conversation is animated. The adults exchange most of the words as my princess keeps studying her future husband, a fascinated smile stitched on her face. His pale blue eyes look around, like he's mapping everything inside his head. I keep trying to guess what he might be planning.

Agatha walks into the room. Her red face flecked with sweat, and the dress she's changed into, is powdered with patches of flour. She bows and approaches her king.

"Apologies, my lord, but Cassandra has fallen ill. I will be serving your meal this evening."

"Of course, Agatha, we look forward to your company." He smiles at her with such ease, and my stomach twists. Where is this love for the rest of his people?

Agatha's face flushes a deeper red, but she squares her shoulders and walks tall. She is a proud woman. She is a good one too.

She enters the hall a few moments later. The smell of her bread leaks around the room. She hands out the slices carefully. She is not an agile woman. Her burly figure bounces around the table.

"Watch it," the prince calls and she flinches back. He corrects and smiles, but his eyes remain icy.

"Excuse me, your highness." Agatha bows her head, her lips quivering.

"Just a mistake." He makes a show to wipe the shoulder where her bosom grazed and smiles at her.

She nods and mumbles another apology before rounding the table and reaching for the service trolley carrying the stew she had been preparing since morning. His cold eyes follow her every move as she ladles the soup into bowls and sets them before the king and queen and then his parents.

She pours the stew into his bowl. Steam wafts as she approaches him. I watch his face. He smiles. He's talking but not to anyone in particular. His eyes are locked on Agatha. Her movements are tentative and stiff, thoughtful and careful. He waits like a coiled snake behind a rock. As she nears him, I realise what he plans, and yet there is nothing I can do about it but watch and seal my ears. Agatha reaches over to place his bowl before him and he sets out his arm at just the right time, sending the scorching soup across her lower face and bosom.

She screeches, the sound agonised and shrill as she falls to her knees. Boiled meat sinks into her blistering flesh as the liquid saturates her dress and meanders through the cracks of her skin, singeing and burning everything in its path. Dolores screams her name and the queen grabs her child and hides her face while the prince apologises profusely for this accidental misfortune. Agatha sinks farther to the floor, her waning wails harrowing and strained as they bleed painfully from her mouth, her red raw chest like a scrap of meat. The king, horrified and disturbed, instructs two guards to take Agatha to be tended to.

The prince keeps apologizing. He seems shaken, yet I know the evil that dwells behind his eyes and his words are swallowed up and ingested by the blind adults.

The mess is cleaned and their dinner is resumed. Dolores' cheeks are streaked with tears and her face marred with worry. She doesn't smile at the prince anymore.

That night I can't sleep. I lie in my cot and listen to Agatha's whimpering.

The guard follows behind them silently. Dolores is excited. I can tell by the way her hands flail around when she talks and the bounce in her step. The prince looks bored as she shuffles along.

Dolores spots me and breaks into a run. She jumps up and I have no choice but to put my hands out and catch her. She wraps her arms around me and I hold her for a second. Though my heart aches, I scold her. "Your prince is here, remember your etiquette."

She groans and huffs, her hot breath fanning my cheek before she hops off. The prince has caught up and eyes me with his cold eyes.

"And who might you be?"

Dolores looks at my face. "He doesn't speak."

The prince smirks at me and nods. "And what are you doing hugging a dumb boy?"

"He's not dumb, he's my friend."

The prince sniggers and his eyes rake along my face like he's trying to see what I look like without skin.

The truth of the matter is that I do speak, I always have, but somehow at the beginning all my words were swallowed up by pain and later by other people's ignorance. Soon I learned, though, that when you do not speak, people think you can't hear and they open up. They fill silences with confessions thinking they would never come to light. One day they all will.

"Your friend?"

Dolores nods and stands a little taller, though she only reaches the top of my hips. My body burns with delight, but I bite my cheek to keep myself from smiling.

"Well, shall we go play?"

He draws out the word and though Dolores jumps and bounds, a shiver trickles down my spine.

"Yes." She grabs his hand and he allows it, like it belongs

to her, and my body ignites with green angry flames. My shallow breaths designed to calm me only flare the fire inside.

"You, boy, join us." His voice suggests I have no choice in the matter. I follow behind them, tempering my irritation.

She brings him to our meadow and her short frame is swallowed up by the long reeds and grass. Just the top of her head bobs as she bounces next to her prince.

"Let's play hide and seek," she calls out excitedly. It's her favourite game and so easy for her given her length and that of the grasses around us and, yet, despite her size and the fact that all she would ever have to do is duck, she always hides behind the same rock. And we go through the same routine.

I lurch around heavily and grunt moving the swaying stalks. The breeze carries her giggles through my body, where it binds with my bones. Then I jump before her and she squeals before falling with laughter onto her back and moaning that I always find her.

"Hide and seek is boring," the prince tells her. "How about a new game?"

"A new game?" Dolores shrieks. "What sort of game?"

"Let's play soldiers." The prince smiles at her sweetly and her eyes grow large and her smile stretches.

"How do we do that?"

"Find some sticks," he tells her.

They search around as I watch. I do not like this idea. Everything feels wrong and yet Dolores is delighted.

"I've got some," she calls out and comes back with some fallen branches. "What do we do now?"

"Should we show her, *boy*?"

Discomfort swells in my gut and I shake my head.

"Go on, let's show the princess how it's done." He smiles encouragingly, and Dolores looks at me, her eyes begging silently, her beautiful features taut with curiosity.

I tip my head and Dolores claps before handing me the

long branch. I point to the rock and she nods, perching herself onto it.

"Ready, princess?"

She nods and he attacks, his branch smashing against mine, sending shivers through my hand that ripple through my body. I tighten my grip, my knuckles bleached white anticipating his next hit as he slashes through the air and brings his branch down onto mine. The crack of wood on wood echoes in the meadow and Dolores shrieks. Maybe in fright, maybe in delight.

The prince smiles and his frosty gaze locks on mine. I can see his intent now as his branch slices the air and beats against mine. I am yet to strike back.

"Come on, boy, play," he urges me on. I know what he wants, but I will not take his bait. Irritation flashes across his face as his branch smacks against mine once again.

The prince sighs and puts down his branch and, leaning on it, he turns to Dolores. "You need to tell your friend to play, or we won't be able to show you how it's done."

My grip tightens around the branch as anger floods my veins and my heart kicks up as it flares inside me.

Dolores turns to me, her eyes focused and annoyed. She folds her arms across her chest and her hips shift to one side. "Do it properly. I want to see. Please?" She softens her demand.

She doesn't know what she's asking, but her pleas wrap around my heart and crush my resolve.

I squeeze my eyes shut and I let out a long exhale. When I open them again, I face the prince and nod. He smirks like he's just won a victory and immediately advances. His branch carves through the air and he swings at me with full force. I defend his blow and push back. He sneers as I do and swings again. I catch his branch with mine and swing to the left as hard as I can, the movement forces the branch from his hand and he releases it. His branch sails through the air and lands in a soft thud, disappearing amongst the reeds. I hold my branch inches from his face, my heart ricocheting in my chest, and my lungs burn. I enjoy my victory and my lips tip up despite my efforts to contain my glee.

Dolores claps and cheers us on. The prince glares at me, wrath smouldering behind his cold eyes.

He smiles and steps backwards, then looks about the meadow, unmoving. "It seems as if I have lost my branch." He shrugs and turns to our accompanying guard. "Give me your sword."

The guard stands stock-still, motionless.

The prince takes a small step towards him. "I said, give me your sword."

He hesitates for another second before unsheathing his sword and handing it over. His face fully covered by his helmet hides all but his eyes that remain emotionless and empty.

I steel myself and wait, as the prince moves the sword around in his hand, its weight challenging his strength as it dips towards the ground. He grips the hilt with both hands and his eyes flash to mine, his face set in a maniacal smile. He looks like a hungry wolf that's just discovered a wounded deer. I swallow the hard lump in my throat and wait, snatching a look at Dolores. Her mouth is set in a tiny 'O', her eyes large and round.

I readjust my grip on my branch and brace. I know the first strike is coming and it will be brutal. He hacks the air, bringing the sword down hard. I slide sideways and the sword flings wildly in his arms. He resets, adjusting his weight, and swings. My branch intercepts the blow, but the sharp blade snaps the wood in half. It dangles limply in my hand. Dolores claps and cheers once more.

The prince bows and she laughs. I keep watching his every move. My fingers tingle and I gulp down my breath. It's not over. I can't let my guard down.

"Did you like that, princess?"

"Yes." She beams, bouncing on her heels.

"Would you like to see me win?"

He doesn't wait for her answer. Instead, he charges, swinging his weapon recklessly, before he lands his strike. It's brutal and heavy and the pain slices through my face as the blade cuts through it like an axe through sinew.

The scream is shrill and pierces the meadow. Somewhere in the distance a flock of birds take flight and caw into the blue sky. I do not know who made the sound, Dolores or me. Or perhaps we felt the agony of the blow at the same time, somehow connected. The thought strengthens and weakens me all at once.

I do not wish for Dolores to see me like this, broken and wounded. Somewhere in the angry buzzing that swims around my head is *his* voice, mumbling apologies, feigning regret.

Hot liquid trickles down my neck and back. The red stains ink across my shirt like a river at sunset. The sharp pain stings my face and tears well behind my eyes as I slurp for more air.

Dolores is crying. Her sobs slice my heart and lacerate it like a sharp sword. I want to comfort her, to tell her that everything will be ok, but instead *he* has his arms around her, her little face nuzzled into *his* chest while he lathers his lies on her, sweet words of apology and warm, comforting hugs. He promises her that I'll be looked after, cared for and when, at last, she relents, he sends her away with the guard, who had remained rooted to his spot since our arrival.

He watches them go before he kneels beside me. His cold eyes glare at me and his face is set in a harrowing scowl. Fear sets its hooks into my hollow gut and tugs, but the fear is not for me, but for Dolores, for my present is her future, one I'm still too weak to protect her from.

"Stupid, stupid boy." His voice slithers and crawls over me

like a swarm of insects. "Don't ever think that you are better than me, or that you can have what's mine." He pauses and runs a hand under his chin as if he expects to find sprouted growth on the smooth skin. "I have worked too hard to earn my place here, to be more than just the fifth son of a monarch so loved by his people I was only ever going to be a part of his shadow."

His mouth twists in a feral snarl. "He only has love for them. Love," he spits out the word. "It's his weakness, one I will never share. When I am king, they will fear me, respect me, they will never think they can take what's *mine*."

He stares into my eyes for a few beats, the frosty blue turning colder with each passing second. There is nothing good inside those eyes. He is like a sea on a stormy day—he can only destroy.

"Dolores doesn't need friends, she has me."

With that he pushes off, using my battered face as leverage. "Great, now you've made my hand dirty," he growls and wipes it over my shirt before cocking his leg and landing a harsh kick into my ribs. The breath spills from my lungs and they crush my chest, strangling me. I can't find air and I choke on the blood and saliva that lodge in my throat.

He turns to leave and I lie still. Somewhere a frog croaks and insects chirp. Cool wind slices through my wound and I gasp. My heart skitters and chugs in my chest. A bird caws in the distance and the earth feels cold against my cheek.

I roll onto my back, the sun kissing my face, but her kisses are no longer sweet or warm, and the grass no longer feels like a blanket, it is a stained bloody carpet that reeks of failure and weakness.

When I'm able, I stagger back to my room where Agatha cowers, still nursing her own wounds. She gasps when she sees me and tends to the gash on my face.

That night we both whimper in the darkness.

CHAPTER FIVE

Ten years later

"Come on," she whispers and waves me forward as I scamper over to her. We are crouched behind the pole, hidden in the darkness. This close to her I can smell her flowery earthy scent. She's never smelt like the rest of them, of cloves and oranges and lavender. She's always been the girl who ran in the meadows with me.

She runs through the shadows to the hidden door and pulls. It opens easily and we sneak inside. Dolores smiles wildly at me and her eyes glint with mischief. She runs up the narrow steps, biting down her laughter. I follow behind.

"Up here, quick," she calls and I use my shoulder to push open the door above us. It flips open and cold air rushes inside and sweeps across my face. Beside me Dolores gasps but doesn't slow down.

"Help me," she whispers, her body waving about like an ocean, constantly in motion. The excitement filters through her and drips over to me.

I kneel before her and lace my hands together, anticipating her touch. When she grips my shoulder, her foot lands on my hands and I push her up. A flurry of hair tickles my face and a whispered giggle echoes down to me as she grabs the roof and pulls herself out of the opening.

I stand and reach till my fingers trace the edge of the small opening, then grip the frozen tiles before pulling myself up and through the opening. The cold sweeps away my breath and I take a step onto the roof. The light smattering of snow has melted under the lazy afternoon sun and has left the tiles glistening and slippery.

Dolores steps away. Her breath escapes her and hangs in clouds before her face. She whips her head around to face me and her wide grin sets my insides on fire.

I wrench my eyes away, scolding myself once more. In the last few years Dolores has bloomed, no longer a child but well on her way to becoming a woman, and each time I find myself around her my body feels different, tighter and harder, burning with need, hijacked with desires I had no right to feel.

"This way." She smiles at me and my traitorous body hardens uncomfortably. I have no control over the tight discomfort in my pants as she flips her long hair over her shoulder, her lips full of invitation.

I follow as he draws nearer to the edge. To the place where we sit and stare over the land and beyond the wall, to the place where she tells me her dreams and her hopes as queen, to the place where she takes those hopes and throws them away to shatter at the foot of the palace, for we both know that that future doesn't exist for her. Yet, like the stubborn woman she is, she holds onto her dreams.

I follow in her wake, fearful of the thoughts and forbidden cravings that swell inside my body, while she glides before me, free and uninhibited by her worries, for her future is sealed and she is free like a bird that escapes the winter cold. But Dolores can't escape. Her wings have been cruelly clipped off by the man who marked my face so viciously. Each time she looks at me I see it in her eyes. I'm a reminder of what's to come, and each time the light in her eyes dims, my heart falls to pieces.

"Come look," she calls and I step closer. "Just a little farther—"

She doesn't finish. Instead, she lets loose a blood-curdling scream that rakes like shards of glass against my heart. Her hands begin to flail and she reaches into the empty air. Her body teeters backwards and her face falls, fear draining away her colour and gravity yanking at her waist.

"Dolores!" I scream for her and lunge. My hands reach and grasp a thin wrist. Her weight yanks against me, but I hold her and her body slams into the wall. A huffed groan meanders from her slightly parted lips like a sad trickling river. She hangs in my grasp, her eyes wide, her limp body tightening with terror.

I pull, clawing and drawing her back over the ledge, ripping her to me, forcing her back from the abyss.

"Dolores." My hands cup her face and my eyes search for wounds or blood, any sign of injury. Her milky skin glistens with sweat and melted snow that has skated over her, my hands rush over her and before I can stop myself she is encapsulated in my arms, my heart pounding, smashing through my chest, trying to reach for hers. My breathing ragged and torn, my body covered in sweat from fear and exertion.

"Dolores," I breathe out her name as I push her away and my hands are back at her cheeks, my eyes locked with hers as the adrenaline trickles away and the fear of what could have been settles like a hard rock inside me.

"You're speaking," she murmurs through chattering lips.

"Dolores." It's the only thing I can think to say. I want to keep touching her, to make sure she is safe, but her face twists and her fear dissolves to tears, which leak down her flushed cheeks.

I draw her to me and her tears burn against my skin. When I release her, her glistening eyes study my face. "You can speak?" Her broken whisper hacks through the thunder in my head.

I nod. "Dolores." Her name tastes like honey on my parched tongue. My voice husky and unrecognisable.

She pushes away from me, her face flooded with wonder and anger. "This whole time?"

We stare at each other, the daylight fading away. Wordlessly I pull us farther from the edge and settle on the wet roof. The moisture has soaked into my clothes and the cold wind stings my skin, but my body burns for Dolores.

We fall onto our backs and silently watch tendrils of darkness chase away the sun, inking the sky in dark blue.

"Do you have a name?" Her voice slashes the silence like a sharp blade.

I shake my head. If I did once I do not remember what it might have been. Soon I hope it will become a number, like the rest of the guards here. I've never mastered the art of pastries, much to Agatha's disappointment, but I, like Dolores, have changed. My long black hair falls to my sloping shoulders and I stand almost as tall as the king himself. When winter flees and spring sprouts I shall begin my training.

"I want to hear your voice," she whispers. It's a tainted soft plea that scrapes at my insides.

"I came from over the wall," I say, getting used to the words that want to tear themselves from me. A gush of unspoken push against the barrier that has been keeping them locked away for so long, aching to get out.

"What's it like there?" She rolls onto her elbow and her keen eyes try to see inside me.

"There is hunger." I don't elaborate.

"You need to take me there." Her eyes light up and grow big, as if her curiosity has struck a match inside her.

I sit and study her face, knowing that her mind is already made up and all my future arguments will fall on deaf ears. She's yet to grow out of her youthful stubbornness.

"You need to get back now. They will be looking for you soon."

She nods, but I know we're not done.

We slink back down the stairs and loom in the long dark shadows. I grab her arm before she scampers off to her room and I pull her to me till her scent invades my insides and light strands of her hair tickle my upper lip as I whisper my own plea, "Dolores."

Her eyes flick from my hand on her arm then to my eyes. "I know." She brings a single finger to her soft mouth before her fingers feather over my hand and I release her.

I watch her creep away in the darkness, carrying my secret.

Dolores has been hounding me. I don't mind her presence so much as her relentless questions. Now that she has found my voice, she wants it constantly, but she asks questions I can't give her the answers for.

She slides up against the pole, keeping her back glued to the stone. I stay hidden in the shadows on the other end, but she knows where I am. She knows too many of my secrets now.

"I want to go tonight," she says on a soft breath.

"No," I answer her in my hoarse voice. Still getting used to the way it scraps my throat as it rolls out of me.

She shrugs and inches closer, her smell intoxicating, and I want to run. She is my weakness and I need to keep away from her, for my own protection. "If you won't take me, I'll go alone."

Her voice is even and determined and I know her mind is set, her stubbornness as hard as the stone pole on which we lean.

I sigh and squeeze my eyes shut for a moment. "Meet me at the tree by the old gate after the third star is out."

I can't see her face, but I sense the smile that rises on it like the sun. Her hand creeps around the pole and brushes over mine, a whisper of a sensation, but I feel it everywhere. "Thank you." The thrill in her voice quakes through me.

And then she's gone.

We shouldn't be here. I should not be allowing this, but she will go, with or without me. And I am her protector. She's left me no choice.

Her shadow scampers across the yard and she comes to rest by me, her short breaths hanging in the air. Her anticipation buzzes around her like a disturbed hornet's nest.

"Follow me."

I bolt towards the old gate, the oversized upper hinge broken atop the crumbled wooden gate, leaving it hanging precariously on a single hinge, creating a small opening through which we sneak out of the palace.

Dolores stops and inhales, as if the air smells differently beyond the gate. Maybe it does and I don't remember, but my heart thumps too loudly and I fear that it will get us caught, so I grab her by the wrist and pull us away, towards the lights in the town below.

Red dust kicks up as we scamper along the abandoned dirt road and towards the growing hum of the town. Trees and shrubs thin out and in their stead we find buildings and firelight, the stretch of humanity rising to greet us.

We step into a different world and the awe is written across Dolores' face. She studies everything around her, while I can't help but examine her features. I watch the marvel climb up her chest, then her neck, landing in her throat and releasing with a delighted gasp.

The darkness—pushed away by firelight—is scattered in drums throughout the street. It lights up the night, bouncing from face to face and settling into crevices as we walk. It dispels the winter chill, our cold skins stinging as we walk by the dancing flames.

The market blooms upon the street like flowers spring from the cracks of cobblestones. I bustles with hawkers and stalls. Men shouting, exchanging bargains, women herding their families to bed, children running in the light snow and catching the flakes on their tongues. They are skinny, and they forget that they are hungry or maybe that's all they think about as the snow touches the tips of their tongues.

She gawks, taking it all in like it's the first time she's used her eyes. The smells of rotten food and freshly cooked seasoned rice assault my senses and my body twirls with memories. For a moment I falter. I remember the streets, though they look different now, not cleaner, but somehow narrower as if people and houses have overflowed into the already cramped space.

A group of lanky children rush by. They laugh and shriek and flutter Dolores's coat. She laughs with them, their excitement running through her.

"Show me where you grew up." She looks up at me and my eyes fall away.

"Nothing to see." I pull her away towards a bread stall. This place feels so similar, and warm, away from the cold stone of the palace and the endless silence. There is so much life here. I forgot. But then life thrives whenever you are close to death, and down here without food and sanitation, we are, we were, I no longer belong to this world.

"Show me anyway." She flattens me with a sweet smile and curious eyes and my insides shudder.

"This way." I jut my chin towards an alleyway. It's dark and bleak as it's always been, the blackened walls still charred from the fire that took everything away.

We walk in the darkness. It envelopes us like a secret and Dolores steps closer to me, her proximity like a breath of hot wind along my skin. I shiver.

The building stands half ruined just as it always has. Parts of its skeleton ruptures from the black earth as if an artist sketched it in charcoal. Fabrics hang from a doorway to the left, sealing a family inside, where I know they huddle together to keep from the cold. New, clean brick has been added around the ruined space that used to be my home, and yet it remains abandoned. Like my childhood, all that's left is ashes.

"This is where you grew up?"

I nod.

"Do you have any memories?"

"I remember hunger," I say solemnly and my mind drifts to nights where the pain gnawed away at me, so harsh and sharp it almost made me forget about my parents.

"Do you have any good memories?"

I search her face, but it's hidden in the shadows, so my eyes drift back to the room that accommodated my frail body and cradled it in the dark nights when my own mother couldn't.

"I used to have a mother but have no recollection of her anymore. I don't remember her voice. It's the thing I lost first, then her eyes and the way her skin used to smell." I shrug. "The best memory I have was the day you were born."

"Me?" She beams.

"Yes. It was the day that everything changed."

"How?"

She asks and my body quakes. I want to tell her it's the

day where my hate turned to love, the day that my heart began to burn, the day I knew I would always belong to her —but I don't.

Instead, I run a hand over my face and shrug. "It's the day I knew I'd join the guard."

I sense her smile. It radiates happiness and washes over me like a hot yellow wave. "So you can always watch over me?"

I swallow the rock lodged in my throat. It keeps a lid on all the emotions boiling inside of me. I wish I'd kept my mouth shut. I nod, hoping she sees the gesture in the dimness that hides the strain around my eyes and the thin line of my mouth.

A sharp chink steals my attention and my head snaps towards the shadows, searching the sordid darkness. Dolores jumps and reaches for my arm. Her fingers dig into my flesh. I stand before her and she shields herself with my body. My heart swells and drums and scampers all at once.

The shadows change. They move and elongate as something approaches. They use the veil of darkness as a weapon, striking fear inside the unsuspecting. Her grip tightens around my arm.

"Don't be afraid. I won't let anything happen to you." She squeezes again, but this time it's understanding, trust. She believes me.

When they are near enough, I can make out three shapes. Tall and lanky, their bodies mere bones covered in a thin layer of skin that drips from them like stretched dough.

We stand in a silent exchange, as their forlorn faces and broken eyes study us.

"You don't belong here." The tallest of the three slices the heavy silence.

When I do not respond, he continues stepping closer. "What do you want?"

"This was once my home," I say, my gaze flickering

between the three men who do not seem much older than I am.

The man snickers and steps closer as I take one back, pushing Dolores with me. "Only ghosts lived there."

My jaw ticks. He's not wrong. The boy who lived amongst the ashes died at the palace under the hooves of a horse.

"We're hungry," the boy states. "You seem well fed."

I know of the hunger he speaks, not only of the insidious pain that cripples the senses and gnaws at your soul, but the ruinous of wanting more than the hand life has dealt.

"I cannot help you." I retreat yet again.

"What are you hiding?" the boy asks and his companions begin to slowly wing us, Dolores sure to be discovered.

"Nothing that can be of use to you," I say, as Dolores' nails spear the skin on my arm.

"Perhaps you should let us see for ourselves. Down here everything holds value, even the rags you wear."

I slither my hand over Dolores' wrist and lock it tight in my grip. Her body tightens behind me like a coil ready to spring.

They inch closer.

"Whatever you do, Princess, once we start running, do not stop," I whisper over my shoulder and tighten my grip. At my words, they halt for a second before they advance at full speed.

I wait, my breath collecting in my lungs like a lead balloon, painful and heavy. My legs ache with tension and my jaw grinds. They close in and I burst forward, yanking Dolores behind me. She staggers and collides with one of the men as I shoulder our way through the pack, knocking the leader to the cobblestones at our feet.

I do not turn around, nor do I slow down as I drag my princess out of the alley and into the street where firelight dances off her golden hair for all to see. My body rams through bodies and mud splashes up, caking my pants and shoes. We run. A sheen of sweat coats my skin as softly as new spring rain. My heart drums in beat with my feet as they hit the path beneath. Dolores' heavy breaths trail behind me, but I do not stop, not when the shouts have died away, or when the fires no longer light our path, nor when I spot the castle walls.

We push through the broken gate and relief floods me as we step over the manicured green lawn loomed over by seemingly impenetrable stone walls. No one can hurt her here. *Yet.* The thought spears through me like a poisonous arrow.

Dolores is pale and breathless and her grey eyes glisten like polished marble. "I was so scared," she utters a frayed whisper.

"Shh." I surrender and graze my knuckles against her cheek, catching an errant tear. "We're fine. I'll never let anything happen to you."

Dolores raises her hand to touch mine. Her fingers feather over my knuckles. The touch makes my body hum and spin, and I have to grind my teeth, as she nudges my hand open and nuzzles into my palm as if it's the most natural thing in the world to do. I want to snatch it away, to disconnect, to tear down the buzzing hive that's come alive inside of me, but then she kisses my palm and my world implodes.

Her hand rises to my face and then without warning the pads of her fingers find my skin. It is but a small thing, being touched, but perhaps not so when your skin cannot remember affection.

Her fingers move slowly, almost lovingly over the scar, then make their way to my lips where they rest softly for only a moment. I close my eyes. My heart dangles in my chest.

"I was so scared," she repeats in that broken voice and the part of me that burns for her sets me alight.

Tearing her hand away in fear of doing something foolish, I pull her into me, clutching her body and letting her head fall against my chest. My hands wrap around her and my fingers find the long strands of her silky hair. They can't help themselves, they intertwine and lace through her long locks and I inhale her, flowers and earth and ash.

I want to say so many things, as her tears soak my shirt and her body quivers like harp strings, but I don't. I continue to stroke her delicate face and let my fingers slide through her hair while holding her to me, till her breathing becomes even and steady.

"You must go now, Dolores."

She nods against my chest and rips herself away, ripping my heart as she does. She gifts me with a fragile smile and I watch as she disappears into the palace, fuelling the fire that rages through my body to consume itself.

CHAPTER SIX

Dolores isn't smiling when they tell her the prince is due for his annual visit. Instead, her eyes travel the length of the hall and land on me. I watch her mouth twist and my heart flinches in my chest. Through my helmet I can focus only on her, cutting out the rest of the room.

My armour is heavy, hot and uncomfortable, but I carry it with ease, because it weighs less than the burden of my secret and because it allows me endless time with my princess. Time to watch over her.

She's no longer the child I played with in the fields but has long ago discarded all the features of her childhood. She has the trappings of womanhood, her curves have filled out, and her budding chest peaks under her dress. Her changing body draws me further under her spell, making mine burn with heat and need which swells uncomfortably between my legs—demanding release—desperate for ways to surrender to the pleasure lurking inside.

Despite her maturity, the world still excites her, but she never outgrew being a hurricane. From the time of her birth she was the eye of her own storm. Her stubbornness and determination embedded under her skin, as was her kindness and passion. From the moment she knew of my secret she kept it as her own and allowed me my time. And when I was ready, she would ask questions and would listen.

There's beauty in being a good listener, someone who seeks to make connections and see things from new perspectives. Which is why she could no longer stand her father.

The king is talking animatedly. He's excited. He's been living in a future that hasn't happened yet and thinks he can avoid. He's certain that he's saved his daughter by giving her away to a monster, when all he's done is doomed her. He's forgotten how to listen. Instead, her wants and needs travel over him while he blindly reassures her that he's already fixed what's broken. He believes that he's the one responsible for saving her.

In time, like everyone else, he will realise his error.

"I don't want to marry him." She looks at her father, who laughs in her face. She faces him, her stubbornness rooting her in place, her arms folded across her chest.

"Nonsense, Dolores, he is our saviour and our future. You'll see, in time you will grow to love him, just as he loves you."

At his words, her eyes flash over to me and my heart cramps. The long, ugly scar slicing my face stings with memories and the memory of her fingers brushing over the deep crevice. My grip tightens around my spear as her eyes dart back to her father.

"He loves only himself." She is of course right, but her words come out like those of a petulant child.

"He is a good and kind prince, and he will make this kingdom great with you by his side." Her father dismisses her as he always does and she glares at him, her grey eyes cold and hard as slate.

Shouts in the distance alert the palace. Hounds bay in the courtyard and trumpets take up their high brassy notes, which carry on the wind and twist around me like rope. I square my shoulders and steel my back. The monster is back to lurk inside my castle.

Dolores fidgets and gripes as the commotion grows outside. When the doors fly open, her eyes shift to mine, searching, perhaps for strength, perhaps for answers, perhaps for the truth we share. We hold each other's gaze until he steps into view, cutting our eyeline and severing our connection.

He walks over to Dolores and takes her hand in his. He bows and charms her with a vivacious smile before grazing her hand with his lips. My heart churns in my chest as I watch. Her mouth lifts in a forced smile and she snatches her hand away as soon as he releases it. A ghost of a smile tugs at my lips as she wipes her hand on the back of her dress.

The king and queen invite him to sit for a drink, to quench his thirst from his long journey. He accepts the invitation, but his eyes are yet to leave Dolores, and I recognise the kind of thirst he wishes to quench, one that makes your throat itch and your body burn and only she could relieve. My jaw clenches and sweat pools at my back.

Agatha walks into the great hall, a basket of freshly baked bread in her shaking hands. The smell wafts and fills the cold space, but it's the terror in her eyes that keeps me cold. Her brisk walk halts and her body quakes as her gaze lands on the prince. He greets her with nonchalance, not recognising the deformed woman before him. Her skin like cracked bread that's been left in the oven too long, lumpy, dry, and taut, full of branching ridges that stuck together unevenly as her skin regrew.

She places the basket down and makes a hasty retreat. Her eyes find mine for a second before she does, and her horror flickers to pride, if only for a second.

I tune out the words and watch only my princess, her long gulps, the way her hands jerk and waver adjusting herself in her seat constantly. Her discomfort radiates across the room and I want to rescue her. But the moment has not yet arrived and so all I can do is keep watching.

"I would like to share a room with my bride-to-be," the prince informs the king. His graceful hand hovers over Dolores. She snatches it away, her large round eyes imploring her father silently.

"She's not yet come of age." The king's words are sharp and crisp in the room.

"Indeed she is not." The prince nods. His eyes track her changing body, taking in all her new curves and contours. She squirms beneath his glare, and he chuckles at her discomfort. "We can share a room but not a bed, and three chamber maids can be present to attest to the fact that she remains untouched."

The king glances at his wife, whose lips are pressed into a thin line.

"No," Dolores interjects, answering for them.

The prince turns to her, his face a pleasant mask hiding the ugliness below. "You are to be my wife in just three short years. Let us get to know one another, discuss our future."

"It will be arranged," her father answers on her behalf and her forthcoming protests fall on deaf ears, ignored as if she was nothing but a barn fly.

Her eyes find mine. They glisten with unshed tears and I want nothing more than to run to her, but we are locked in place, her on a wooden throne and me inside my armour that with each passing moment feels more like a prison, closing in on me. I shift my weight, rattling invisible chains.

The prince and the king keep talking as if the rest of the room has vanished. They make plans for a future that hasn't happened yet and doesn't include Dolores or her dreams. It irks me.

The king shares his kingdom with his wife, they speak of matters together and she weighs in on important matters, and yet he dismisses his daughter as if she is a burden and not the blessing he and his wife prayed for year after year.

My thoughts churn inside me, mixing with the dripping disdain for the king and the cuffs he's placed upon my princess.

The party breaks up, and they scatter to their chambers to freshen up and get ready for the evening's dance, yet I stand at my post, fixed in place like a statue, and watch her go where I cannot follow, where I cannot protect her, or reach her. My coveted status in the king's guard which was meant to give me power has rendered me completely useless.

The hall has been transformed. Flowers hang and candlelight from the chandeliers above flickers across the high ceiling. Perfumed men and women gather around tables loaded with food and ale like animals at a watering hole.

Dolores floats among them. They part for her, then close around her like ripples. She is a rock in their river, making everyone move around her. She smiles and greets them all in turn, making time for each of them. Making them all feel special and important, making them feel her equal. But I know, no one can ever be her equal—no one will ever come close.

The night is full of laughter and dancing, courteous smiles and cups full of mead. But under the music there is constant noise, a hum of voices all talking of the handsome prince in their midst. All noting his broad shoulders and sun-kissed hair, his delightful smile and sky-blue eyes. It is because they haven't seen him turn to ice yet.

He approaches Dolores. Her eyes fall to the floor and her happiness sheds away like winter snow off branches. Her colour blanches as he reaches for her hand and the crowd parts as he leads her to the dance floor. He moves like a howling wind whipping against stone. Her rigid body trapped against his. The song ends, the crowd claps, she escapes him, and her eyes search the room till they find the safety of mine.

Wax drips to the floor as the candles burn away and the mead sinks in beneath skins and moulds to bone, making women's laughter louder and men bolder.

Dolores returns to her throne where she seems to shrink, while the prince walks around the room, learning his new kingdom. He's not like her. Whereas she leaves behind sunshine and smiles, he lives behind a devastating fire. They are like insects, drawn to the heat, to his beautiful flames, but something primal, instinctual within them makes them aware of the danger. If they'll come too close, they'll burn.

He scouts the room till he spots a young lady. She's clad in a dress that hugs her young figure. She can't be much older than my princess and her eyes light up when he approaches. His fingers trace her spine and red stains her face and neck, spreading to her chest like a plague, before her gaze lands on his handsome face. The top of her tongue escapes her mouth and runs along her lip. He smiles and leads her to the dance floor where they twirl and swing.

The prince pulls her to him. His hand slips and slithers till it lands on her buttocks. Her face falls and tightens and still he draws her in further. He whispers in her ear and her eyes grow round and frightened like an animal caught in a dangerous trap. She shakes her head and his blue eyes ice over. He whispers again, but his jaw is rigid and his eyes spear her with ice. She crumples under his look and nods, a slight tense movement that sets free a villainous smile across his lips.

The prince makes his way across the room, plucking maidens from the safety of their friends and family and whispering curses in their ears. Each time they follow him willingly and when they leave his arms, they are limp and ragged as if the joy has been sucked out of their very soul. Anger wriggles inside me like maggots and my legs feel heavy, leaden, unable to move. I find solace in Dolores' eyes. She finds me time and again, and we feed off the other's strength. We are two vessels emptying each other in turns.

The candles flicker. Their flames wane till they die out and the dance draws to an end. The ladies and lords return to their homes save a handful of maidens whose presence was demanded by the prince. He lines them up like prized horses and examines each in turn, running his hands through their hair. He draws out the strands slowly between his fingers before tucking them back almost gently behind their ears. His long fingers slither along their cheeks before his thumb slides over their painted lips and smearing the colour around before forcing it into their mouths.

Their ivory skins blotch with red as he slowly pulls it out just to force it back inside again and again. A fiendish smile decorates his face and madness flickers in his eyes as he watches their faces crumble, teary-eyed and quivering. When he's done, he smears their shame on their faces and meanders down their flushed necks, onto their heaving breasts, which he fondles unabashed, eliciting some cries of terror and shame. He searches their faces as he touches them, pinching and stroking relentlessly, till their breaths grow heavy and their eyes grow wide and their shame turns to need. It is then that he lets his hands fall away and he chuckles as he steps away, watching humiliation flood their faces.

My heart slams inside my chest, attempting to drown out the dread. I stand helpless, useless, silent, as the prince ends his parade and picks out three maidens from the row of women who have been ruined slowly and delicately before me.

The discarded women run, afraid perhaps that he may

change his mind. I know as well as he does that none shall speak of this happening in fear of retribution, and so he is unconcerned with their rushed escape. He turns to his victims. Evil veils his eyes as he smiles over his cowering brood.

"Let us retire to my chamber," he says, his voice dripping with poison honey. "My princess awaits."

My pulse hammers at the notion.

"No," one whispers, the tremor in her voice palatable.

"No?" the price asks, a single eyebrow arching over an arctic expression.

"No." She shakes her head.

The prince strikes. His palm connects with her cheek and she yelps, as her skin turns bright red. Her hand shoots to her face, but the prince lands another strike, with the back of his hand. She yelps again, cowering.

His foot connects to her back and she falls to the ground where he rains down a barrage of savage kicks. Her screams die down till there is nothing but silence and a limp body lying at his feet. He turns away from her as if she is nothing but dust and trails his fingers through his hair, placing the unkempt strands back into place. He smiles at the other two who clutch each other, their knuckles white, bulging eyes and rasping breaths.

"Shall we?" He puts out his arms like a rooster. The women tear themselves apart and reluctantly weave their hands around his. He gifts them with a charming smile and their tight lips attempt to return it. He chuckles as he leads them away.

In the darkness all my thoughts bond and form a singular painful realisation, the witch was right, but only partially, for my princess is indeed cursed, but I can do nothing to save her.

From beyond the sealed room there are only agonised screams. I cannot decipher the voices. They break against my body and shatter, nicking at my heart. I bleed for them in silence.

When I am relieved of my shift, the screams have dwindled to mere desperate whimpers. I skulk away, haunted by the thoughts of the broken puppy.

The cold air bites at my skin as I step outside and remove my helmet. I suck in air, but my lungs feel depleted. No matter how much I breathe, I feel suffocated. The dark closes in on me like a noose and I trudge through it, wanting to leave the sounds of mystery behind me.

"Wait!" Her voice slices my dark thoughts and I look up to see her running across the grounds. Her blue dress swoops over the grass like waves. She catches me mid stride and I study her face, wild and damp with tears.

"What are you doing here, Dolores?" My whisper comes harsher than I intended and she flinches away.

"I'm afraid." Her body shivers and wracks against my heart.

I squeeze my eyes shut and inhale, and my lungs finally fill with air and earth and flowers and Dolores. I snap my eyes open and lock my hand around her wrist, dragging us to the safety of the shadows, beneath the cold stone walls that keep everyone's secrets.

"Did he hurt you?"

She shakes her head, but tears spring to her eyes and leak down her cheeks, and her pain coils around me like thorns until I feel it too. She clings to me like there's anything I can do, like I mean more to her than I should, and my heart clenches with vicious hope as I flush away the feelings that try to swell inside me.

"Did he hurt them?"

She nods. "He is not a good man." Her voice quivers, stating a truth we've both known for years.

My teeth grind together and anger rises inside me like a tide, but my hands are tied in heavy invisible chains that render me useless.

"I won't let him hurt you." I promise her, knowing that I intend on keeping my word, whatever that may mean.

Her head leaves my chest and our gazes meet, locking. Something potent and forceful passes between us. She raises her dainty hand and as before, the pads of her fingertips delicately trace the long, deep trench the prince sliced into my face. The contact, intimate, almost too much to bear. I know I should pull away, but her touch is bewitching and I can't rip my eyes away from hers. So full of questions and secrets.

Then without warning or thought she pushes onto her tiptoes and her lips brush mine, softly, delicately, like butterfly wings, just long enough that I inhale her breath and feel the warmth of her skin.

My body hums and buzzes, and she pulls back before I can so much as protest, or pull her back into me. Her eyes grow wide and her face fills with bewildered curiosity as she looks at my lips, her own pressed together as if she is replaying how they felt on mine.

"Dolores, what have you done?" My heart spins in my chest and I try to get my tapered breath under control.

She chews on her lip for a second as her gaze darts over to the palace. "I'm sorry." She whispers, "It's just that I hate him, and I lov—"

"Don't!" I halt the avalanche of her words.

"But—"

"Please, Princess"—I trail my fingers through my hair, tugging at the roots—"don't say what I think you intend on saying."

"My confession." She whispers.

"My curse." The words taste acrid in my mouth.

A small sob hitches in her throat and tears prickle her eyes once more. "But—"

"No." I harden my tone and my insides. "You can never say those words to me, Dolores, you cannot kiss me again, or hold me, or look at me in the way that you do." The words shred through me as I see her face collapse. They are a rusty knife I aim carelessly at her exposed heart. "I'm a guard in your father's army and will never be worthy of more."

"And what am I worthy of?" Fresh tears cleave her cheeks. "That man in there? Who slices and hurts for pleasure?"

"Dolores—"

"No, you are right," She falls silent as the grey in her eyes clouds over in an angry storm. Stepping back from me, she wipes her tears away with the back of her hand and hides her pain behind a wall of hurt and anger. "Loving you will only destroy me."

She walks away and all I feel is hollow.

I have always thrived on silences, deep and long, but never suffocating, not like they are now. Now the silences stretch endlessly into the unknown and fear nibbles at my feet like waves. Her marble eyes set solid, refusing to meet my own, despite my muted imploration.

I beseech my heart to stop beating for her, begging it to harden, to find other desires. I remind it that my words were true and a princess could never be with a soldier, not in our world, but my heart doesn't care, it doesn't listen, it has stopped talking to the rest of me. Instead, it chooses to drag me to many dark and terrible places. I think it thrives on pain, and the thing about pain, despite the exquisiteness of it —it still hurts.

My shift stretches on like some vast, angry field bending under a fierce wind. I watch my princess as she bestows her gift of laughter and conversation on others, knowing none are reserved for me.

I step away when I am relieved and steal away under the night sky. It glitters with stars and yet even its beauty cannot shake me from my foul mood. I make my way to the clump of trees. They huddle together by the old gate and I lean against the rough bark, wishing to ease my mind, but all my thoughts return to her. The delicate feel of her lips, the collapse of her face, the cool angry eyes and her crushing silence.

A movement distracts me and I jump to my feet, tucking myself between the old trees. The figure slices across the courtyard, tucking itself against buildings and running in the shadows. I recognise her once her hair glistens in the moonlight. I follow her path as she makes her way towards me and I hold my breath as she passes, leaving me undetected.

I watch my princess, as I always do, till she reaches the old gate. She looks around, uncertainty and determination warring on her face before she squeezes herself through the small gap.

Untangling myself from my hiding spot, I dart behind her and push my bulk through the crack that feels as if it has gotten smaller. Far too small. When I'm across, I search the darkness and find her. Back glued to the towering walls, chest heaving.

Dolores doesn't see me until I'm upon her. "Dolores." She jumps at my harsh whisper. "What are you doing?"

"Why do you care?" she throws at me, a sullen voice often reserved for her father.

"You are not allowed out of the castle walls."

"You keep telling me what I am and not allowed to do. You are not my father."

"No."

"I can do what I like."

"We both know that you can't."

"And who are you to tell me what I can and cannot do? You are nothing but a palace guard and I am your princess."

Her words spear me as she tries to push away from me.

I grip her wrist and throw her against the wall where my hands cage her and my eyes seek hers. When she finally holds my gaze, my heart stutters. The marble swirls with anger, no longer a solid lifeless rock.

"Dolores." My voice is an unmistakable warning.

"Let me be, *boy*." She slathers my title with venom.

"No, go home."

"And be condemned to a life with him when all I want is you?" Her hands reach up to my chest and I flinch away. Her mouth twists in agony.

"Don't say that."

"But I do." Her eyes grow like two moons, round and beautiful glittering in the darkness.

"Dolores." I sigh. "You don't know what love is, you are still a child."

Her face hardens and her arms close around her waist. "I know how I feel when I'm around you. I know how my stomach flutters and my heart beats twice as fast and everything feels so much easier, so much better."

"Dolores—"

She ignores me and keeps speaking. "The way your voice echoes through me and your words make me shiver, the way you know what I feel even when I don't. The way you care for me and see me in ways others can't even begin to understand." Her eyes fall away and search the dirt at our feet. "If that's not love, I don't know what is."

I run a hand over my face, hiding the emotions that must surely be surfacing, but our love is doomed, forbidden. Even entertaining such thoughts can have me killed in an instant, and for a moment the thought is sweet. Like the first lick of jam, death would bring such sweet relief.

Her eyes flicker back to mine and tears bite at the edges.

She chews on her quivering bottom lip and I know it is to keep her anguish locked inside. I cup her cheek. I shouldn't. I shouldn't be running my thumb along her jaw or know the depth of her heart.

"Dolores." I wait for her eyes to find mine. "These feelings are forbidden. You must find a way to forget them."

"I don't want to," she whimpers.

"But you must."

"And if I can't?"

I shake my head, having no answer, for I have tried to shed my feelings for her, but all I seem to do is fortify my love with each passing year. I drop my hand and step away from her.

"You are condemning me to him."

My teeth grind and my heart buckles.

"He'll do to me what he did to them. Is that what you want?" Her voice shudders and breaks.

A heart-wrenching sob escapes my princess and her knees buckle. I catch her, but we both fall to the ground, her head to my chest, her hot tears bleeding into my skin. She clings to me and I allow her, this one time.

"Tell me what the prince did." And she does between gasps and sobs. She tells me how he sliced their skin and painted their lips red with their blood. How he impaled them forcefully like dogs, how he shackled them like beasts and leered at their mystery. All the while his cold white eyes remained fixed on her.

I hold my princess and let her cry into my chest and promise myself this would be the only time.

The hall feels bigger again. It allows me to breathe now that Dolores looks at me again and remembers I exist in her big world. And yet the feeling tears at me, ripping me in slow bites off the bone. My heart feels too big and too warm and yet all this hope is false and dangerous. Our end has already been written.

Dolores is still young. Her infatuation with me may pass onto another. The thought cracks at my walls and I blow out a long breath, agitation prickling the back of my neck like ants. I want to let her go, I should, and yet the thought of her affection given to another makes everything inside me ache.

But for now as her eyes dart over to me and she gifts me with a splendid smile, I feast on the lie and let it fill me.

CHAPTER SEVEN

Two years later

"I am afraid." Her large eyes look up at me and implore me for help I cannot give. We lean against the dark bricks and I hold her in the darkness.

"I won't let him hurt you," I repeat my promise just as I have on many nights when we'd snuck out beyond the wall and shared our thoughts and secrets.

"Tomorrow is my birthday."

I nod. I have spent sixteen years celebrating the day of her birth in secret, delighted that I have her to love and cherish and protect.

"Tomorrow he moves into my chambers." She releases a heavy sigh. "Mother says a year will give us time to get to know one another and fall in love."

At her words, my chest feels like collapsing, but instead, I inhale and squeeze my eyes shut, hoping to wake to a different reality.

"I got you something," I say, wishing to talk about

anything but him and her sealed in a room together.

"You did?" Her eyes grow large and a smile slides across her face.

I shift my weight and reach into my pocket, pulling out the disfigured parcel, and hand it to Dolores, my body suddenly feeling tight. I rub the back of my neck and watch as her slender fingers pick away at the stained paper.

She pulls out the white rock hung crudely on the too thin necklace I'd fashioned out of dried twine.

"My rock?" She recognises it instantly. Her fingers flutter to her mouth and my pulse kicks up.

"Yes." I bite back a smile that threatens to escape, but her delight is sweet and infectious.

She strokes the smooth white rock with her thumb and her eyes shoot up to mine. "How? I thought that I had lost it that day."

"You did."

"Then how?" Her gaze flicks back from me to the rock in her hand, setting my heart ablaze with each of her captivated looks, threatening to scorch me from the inside and leave nothing of me but a burned out shell.

I remain silent. My head drops back onto the wall and I gaze at the dark sky, thinking of the day she'd lost it.

We played hide and seek in the meadow, the long grass shielding her seven-year-old body from me. Her giggles carried on the wind and gave her away, as they always did. When we lay down, her head rested on my chest. We counted flies and bees and birds before she pulled out the rock. Rounded and polished and foreign. A trader had come into town two weeks prior and showed her father a game. Pieces on a wooden square that moved around in strange patterns, carved out of rocks, ivory, and ebony so dark they were blacker than a bleak winter's night sky.

When she'd tried to reach out for the pieces, her father slapped her hand away, telling her the game was not for children. The trader, having a daughter of his own, produced the rock from his pocket and handed it to Dolores, proclaiming it possessed great magical properties.

She'd carried it everywhere, whispering wishes into its dead core. When our game ended, she dug into her pocket just to find it gone. After hours of searching and an inconsolable Dolores returned to the castle, I returned to the field. I scoured the earth on my knees day after day through blistering winds and unforgiving sunny days, until at last I found it.

I tied the twine around it so that she would never lose it again.

She elbows me, dragging me out of my memory. "How?"

I shrug. "Happy birthday, Princess."

Before I have any time to react, she's in my arms, wrapping herself around me. "Thank you," she whispers into my neck and heat spreads through my body. She presses herself against me and her eyes rise to mine. My forehead dips to hers and we're breathing each other's air.

Having her so close makes my body crave and harden and want things I had forbidden it to want around her, but as her eyes flicker to my lips, she leeches away my strength and I capture her mouth in a soft, gentle kiss that speaks of my secret desire.

Instead of pulling away, I kiss her again, this time deeper, harder. Her hands thread through my hair and I pull her to me, indulging.

My body is betraying my mind. I want it to stop, but I'm powerless against her. My lips and tongue reveal all my secrets, my lust, my longing, my pain, my love, while hers profess the same truths.

I tear away, ripping her face from my hold, and step back. I've already done too much.

"Happy birthday, Princess," I say again and avert my gaze, unable to look at her beautiful flushed face.

She reaches out to me and I flinch away as if she's stung me. Her face balks.

"Please don't," I beg in a broken voice. Doesn't she know that if I look at her again, or touch her again I will not be able to stop myself?

"Thank you, for my gift." She disappears behind the walls and I collapse to the ground, wondering how I will survive the next year.

Dolores is smiling, but she's also lying to everyone in the room. The fear in her eyes doesn't match her upturned lips and the beautiful flower crown weaved into her hair. She wears her new necklace around her neck and my stomach knots as I think of her taste. The room is full of noise and yet she is silent. Laughter, music, and the murmur of voices, a room full of strangers all here to celebrate her seventeenth birthday.

Her father is brimming with joy, for his daughter's saviour has arrived. The prince walks into the hall while the lords and ladies bow, and the king gathers him into his arms and calls him son. The prince smiles, but like Dolores, he is lying. He will save no one but himself. The king leads him to the stage where Dolores stands to greet him. A silent exchange passes between them while they bow and she places her hand in his. His lips linger on her knuckles for far too long and my jaw clenches behind my helmet. She rips it away at the first opportunity, but all he does is chuckle as he laces her hand with his and leads her around the room like a trophy.

He laughs and tells endless stories of battles and horse rides, of matters of state he had resolved and how he plans to win over the princess' heart and rescue us all. They clap and cheer and eat up his words while my hatred slithers inside me like a parasite.

He is no longer a boy, but a man much like his father, broad and fair and strong. His tailored clothes stick to his body and show off his muscular physique as he peacocks around the room. His eyes haven't changed, still cold, still appraising each person he meets like a victim or competition.

With the men he stands tall, his shoulders squared and his sharp jaw uplifted as he talks to them over his nose. A hand on their shoulder closing in slowly, burying fingers in flesh till they buckle and step away, their lesson learned. He moves closer again and his hands wrap around their shoulders. He tells jokes and finds camaraderie in their midst. He is the people's prince, they fear and respect him, though I dread the truth, they do not fear him near enough.

With the women he smiles and tracks their bodies in a slow journey that makes them retreat or swoon. He locks onto their lips before his gaze follows the contour of their necks down to their bosoms where he examines them with great interest, as if it were cake. When he looks up into their eyes again, their cheeks flush red and he winks at them, knowing he has elicited in them forbidden thoughts.

Dolores shivers at his antics and her tight gaze finds mine. Her fear melts away for an instant, reassurance taking its place. But the moment is short-lived, for a breath later I feel another staring at me. I tear my eyes away from my princess and search for the source, to find the prince piercing me with an intent look. His eyes snap from me to Dolores and back again and cold dread spills down my spine, branching slowly into my body.

He disengages himself from the maiden he had trapped in conversation and turns in full, his cold eyes locked on mine. He strolls over, cocky and overconfident, a long smile stretching across his face as he drags Dolores behind him.

She chews on her bottom lip as he comes to a stop before me. Running a hand over his hair, he pushes a lock back into place and appraises me, his gaze seeking to find my face behind my helmet.

He steps closer still, till we are inches apart. His glacial eyes spear me like icicles, yet I do not look down nor step back.

"What is your name, guard?"

I remain silent as I always have.

"Your prince asked you a question." He steps into my space, his chest pushing into mine. I hold his gaze, saying nothing.

"His name is Two Three Six," Dolores pipes up from behind us. "He does not speak."

His head tilts to the side and a malicious smile spreads across his face. "Doesn't speak, you say? The boy who wanted to be a knight is now a guard?" He steps back as laughter erupts from him, a menacing cackle that ends as abruptly as it started. His eyes glaze over with a layer of ice and he steps closer once more.

"Remove your helmet."

I inhale an agitated breath as my heart chugs in my chest, beating like a drum against my armour.

"Now, *boy*." He smears the words and his jaw ticks.

When I pull it off, the malevolent smile returns to his face. "Ah, it is indeed you. The *friend*." He brings his finger to my face, prodding viciously into the deformed cavity before tracing the long scar he branded me with, the nail digging into the flesh, leaving behind a lingering stinging trail.

He steps closer still, till I feel his warm breath on my ear. "I thought I'd already made it clear that my princess doesn't need any friends." His palm closes over my face, the thumb digging into my cheek.

"Do you like what you see when you look at her? Do you like my princess?"

My eyes flick over to Dolores, whose fingers feather over the rock hanging around her neck, and suddenly it seems more like a noose, a curse I have bestowed on her. I remain silent.

"I think you like watching over my princess, don't you?" His hand travels up to my neck and his finger curls in my hair as he speaks. "If you like to watch, I'll give you something to look at."

He pulls slightly away till his hand lands on my shoulder and his cold smile evaporates what heat it had left in my body. "See you soon, *boy*."

He curtsies, setting off a round of laughter from the crowd that had gathered around us. I don't dare look at Dolores as he drags her farther and farther away from me.

The breakfast table sits laden with food and drink as the royal family takes its place around it. Dolores' chair is pushed far too close to that of her prince. The meal is overindulgent and I know the pigs will enjoy a heartier meal than I will before noon. Dolores picks at the food, shovelling it across her plate and back again.

The prince looks over at me, a serene grin on his lips before he turns to the king. "Your majesty," the prince begins. My ears prick up as dread coats my insides.

The king looks up from his meal.

"As you know, I have my own personal guard while I adjust to living in your beautiful home. However, I'd noticed my beautiful Dolores is defenceless, let loose in the castle without a guard."

The king smiles at his future son-in-law. "Your worry is sweet, dear boy, but Dolores is perfectly safe within the walls of the castle."

"And what of outside?"

"Outside?"

"Yes, I would like to take my future bride exploring. No princess should rule without seeing her own country."

The king nods as he scratches his lush beard, which swallows his digit like a hungry beast.

"If you grant me permission, I've already selected the perfect guard to look over my princess." His eyes shoot to me as he speaks. "I have no doubt he would lay down his life for hers."

The king's fingers peek in and out of his beard like worms as he looks at the prince thoughtfully. "As you wish."

Smirking, the prince winks at me before thanking the king.

I suck in a choppy breath and steady my sprinting heart, hoping I can withstand whatever he has in store for me.

The garden is in full bloom. Azaleas, daisies, and jasmine lure the bees and the butterflies and the sun kisses Dolores' face as she leans back on her arm, sitting on the rug. The same sun stews me slowly inside my armour. The prince has arranged a picnic, grapes, peaches, and sweet melon on silver trays that glint beneath the sunshine, an abundance of fruit and bread and cheeses.

I stand at a distance. The light breeze that falls and rises carries only wisps of conversation and my agitation grows as the prince curls his fingers around her long locks and feeds her sweet fruit, kissing away the spilled juice from her chin.

Dolores smiles and laughs, but her body is stiff and her knuckles white as they bury themselves into the rug. I stand like a sentinel, silent and idle, and watch, as I've been told to do, cooking slowly in my shell, being reminded that all I ever was and all I ever would be is utterly useless.

A man approaches from the gate and I stop him in his

tracks as he walks towards the rug. "You may escort him over," the prince instructs and I follow the man as he closes in on the betrothed.

The prince stands up and greets the man with a firm handshake "Master Edward, how good of you to come."

"Of course." The man smiles and his gaze wanders over to Dolores, who sits still clutching the rug.

"Ah." He turns to look at the princess. "I see you have noticed my wife-to-be."

The man nods, still appraising my princess.

"How could you not?" He extends a hand to Dolores and pulls her up beside him, his hand slithering over her waist. "Isn't she the most beautiful woman you have ever seen?"

"Yes, your highness."

"Does she not have perfect contours and features for your work?"

His work? Dread spikes the rhythm of my heart.

"Indeed she does. She will be a pleasure to work on."

The prince's smile stretches across his face. "Indeed, her beauty must be immortalized in one of your paintings."

"It will be my honour, my prince."

"Indeed it will be."

Dolores shifts next to the prince and he turns to her. "Master Edward is the most renowned painter in the land. He is here to capture your youth and your beauty."

A frail smile crosses her face and she dips her head at the artist.

"You will be immortalized in paint and your portrait hung in the great hall for all to admire."

A light pink tinge climbs up her throat and across her face and her head shakes lightly.

"Ah, a beauty that does not know she is beautiful." Master Edward's eyes light up. "So precious."

The prince smirks and nods. "Go and settle in, we begin at noon."

"Yes, my prince." The master turns to leave.

Dolores pushes away from the prince, who still holds her. His fingers carelessly run up and down her arms. "I do not want my portrait painted."

"Why not, sweet princess? Do you not desire for your beauty to be preserved?" He plucks a grape and sucks it into his mouth as he studies her face, his serene and calm, his eyes a warm, inviting ocean.

"My time can be better spent."

"How?"

She chews on her bottom lip and her eyes fall to the ground, searching the perfectly manicured blades of grass.

"Go on, Princess, tell me how."

She meets his eyes, not daring to look elsewhere. "The townspeople, my parents have let them down." She falters and studies his face, perhaps—like me—expecting laughter and ridicule, but it does not come.

"Go on."

"They are starving. They are our subjects. They deserve better than their lot."

The prince scratches his chin. Light whiskers gleam under his fingernails. "You are indeed beautiful, inside and out. Your compassion is admirable. And you are right, dear Dolores, they do deserve so much more."

Her eyes light up as she eats away at the crumbs he throws at her.

"I'll tell you what." He takes her hand in his and strokes it lightly with his thumb, making my skin buzz with discontent. "After you sit for Master Edward, I will personally take you to the town, and together we can converse with our citizens and listen to their ideas."

"Really?"

"I will never lie to you, sweet princess." He brings her hand to his mouth and lays the softest of kisses across her knuckles, his eyes locked on hers.

Pinks stains her cheek as my heart constricts.

She nods and they settle back onto the carpet, which is now shaded and cool. I stand under the sun in my metal cocoon. Sweat stings my eyes and puddles at my feet as it leaks in slow rivulets down my body. I do not fear the harsh sun, nor the prince's cruel game, nor do I fear that my body will crumble, for it will endure the pain, the slow burning torture of the afternoons. It is my heart that troubles me, for I worry it might stumble beneath heartbreak.

The sun moves slowly overhead in a perfectly blue sky, when Master Edward returns to the garden, interrupting the prince while he whispers in Dolores' ear. Her body has long since relaxed and her laughs have been genuine and frequent, like shards of glass scraping on my insides.

The artist sets up a canvas and paints, then takes a pencil and begins to sketch. The black lead leaving behind traces of a face I've etched into my soul long ago. When he is done, he picks up a paintbrush and begins to cover the canvas in crude thick colour, the paintbrush licking the fabric like a lover's tongue on skin.

The master lets his canvas dry and approaches Dolores. He studies her face, her eyes, her soft, full lips and long, flowing locks, which he arrangers around her shoulder and instructs her not to move.

He sits in long silences, contemplating his model before he begins to streak the canvas with paint.

We return day after day to the garden where the sun beats down on me in anger, while Dolores' face appears in more detail against the dark canvas. The master is indeed masterful in his handy work, for he captures not only her beauty but her spirit. And through her eyes I see only pain, fear, and darkness.

On one such day, the master sets aside his brushes and considers Dolores. "What irks you?"

"Why, nothing at all, Master." Her eyes trail the row of flowers and grass till they fall at my feet, not daring to look at me, before she flicks her gaze back to the artist. He nods and closes his eyes, tilting his face towards the sun. When he looks at her again, a content smile adorns his face.

"Think for me of a beautiful memory, Princess."

He waits.

Despite herself, her eyes dart over to me, shining more brightly than the sun ever dared. A sweet, sorrowful look that I have missed, for she's denied me her eyes for weeks, gripped by fear. Her hand reaches for the rock around her neck and a delicate smile touches her lips, making my heart ripple in my chest, sending something akin to happiness I should not be feeling into every part of me.

"There," the master says before he continues his work in silence.

Each night I return to my chamber and remove my scalding armour. Beneath, my body stings, red and hot. It screams for reprieve. I soak in cool waters till the agony fades to a dull throb, knowing tomorrow will bring more pain, more damage.

We spend weeks in the summer garden. My body is a raw, peeling lump of flesh, which each night I soak till the worst of the pain dissipates like fog off a lake. Dolores' face peaks from the canvas, layer upon layer of paint set to dry and re-paint, while she sits like a porcelain doll rooted to her spot in the garden.

The prince spends but an hour with his bride-to-be, charming her and drawing laughter from her stubborn mouth, till the master scolds him and he leaves her there smiling and still.

The overcast sky looms above us in dark shadows when the master declares he has completed his masterpiece. Dolores sits against a stark background. Her beautiful features leap from the canvas and her eyes follow me everywhere.

The prince shakes the master's hand and brings Dolores over. She examines the art work and her face beams. Her mouth falls open in wonder and delight.

"Do you like it, Princess?" the prince asks as he draws her against him.

"It's beautiful." Her surprise is palpable.

"As are you." He kisses her forehead, sending a shiver of anger through me. "Are you happy?"

She nods and her face is a mask of treacherous delight.

The prince places another delicate kiss on her forehead as his eyes land on mine and his lips tug up in a smirk.

"Come in, come in." The prince is pleasant and welcoming as he cracks open the door to their bed chamber. "You too." His smile turns cold. "My princess needs to be watched over."

I follow the master into the room where Dolores looks up from her bed. She's dressed in a simple white sleeping gown, her long hair loose and cascading gently over her shoulder. She looks up at us perplexed and turns to the prince.

"What are they doing here?"

"Why, the master is here to finish his work." He reaches his arm out and she takes it, allowing him to pull her from the bed.

Her brow creases as she looks from the master to the prince. "But he is done."

"No, my dear." He places a kiss on her cheek and runs a

finger along her jaw. "Not yet, not till he captures your true essence."

"I don't understand?"

He chuckles and begins encircling her. His long fingers drag along her shoulder and catch her hair. "My sweet, delicate princess, your beauty does not stop at the line of your clothes, for there is so much more of you to see. Now remove your nightgown."

"My prince?"

"Do you not want to go to the town? Do you not want to help *your people*? Do you not wish for me to keep my promise to you?"

The crease in her brow deepens and my raw skin tingles beneath my armour.

"I—"

"What's wrong, Princess? Have all those days in the garden dumbed down your senses? Strip."

Dolores remains rigid in place, the colour slowly draining from her face.

"Did you not hear me, Princess? Remove your garments or I will remove them for you. The master is here to work, and has no time to waste on spoilt little girls."

Dolores stands pale and shivering.

The prince clicks his tongue and slips his fingers into her shoulder straps before pulling forcefully. The fabric rips beneath the force and the sound echoes in the silent room.

Dolores clutches at the fabric before it falls to the floor, steps away from the prince, and squares her shoulders. She inhales a long breath, squeezing her eyes shut before releasing the fabric, allowing it to fall to the ground at her feet. I look away, refusing to allow the prince to corrupt the thing that is most precious to me.

I feel his presence by me and turn to face him.

"Remove your helmet, Two Three Six."

I shake my head and remain holding his gaze.

"Remove your helmet or I'll invite all the men in your regiment to stand in this room in your stead."

My jaw ticks as I grind my teeth into dust and rip the helmet from my head.

"Good boy." He pats me on the head before gripping my chin. "Now look at her." His voice slithers over me like a leech sucking the soul from my body. "You like watching her, boy, don't you? Now, look."

He turns my head towards Dolores, but my eyes remain on the floor.

"I told you to look!" He hisses over me and my fists clench at my sides. Contrition climbs inside me like thorny ivy.

My eyes flicker to hers, where resignation settles like frost on leaves. My gaze leaves her ashen face dappled in splotches of red and begins to track her body. Flames of fury and desire lick my insides as I take in her long neck, her bare shoulders, and her collarbones. Dread consumes me as I continue down. I'm relieved and ashamed at my disappointment to find her hands covering her breasts.

The prince leaves my side and turns back to her. "Oh, Princess, this will not do. The master must see you. *All* of you." He approaches her trembling shape and takes her hands in his, bringing them to his lips, before he tucks them at her side. His body shielding hers from prying eyes. From *my* prying, hungry, desperate eyes.

She lets out a strangled gasp and the prince takes a small step away. "Yes, much better, sweet princess." He steps around her and gathers her hair in his hands, placing every last golden lock behind her back, revealing all her bare flesh.

I dare not look. I cannot. And my eyes lock on the master, as my body churns with rage and shame. He leers at Dolores. His eyes narrow as he studies her shape and curves free of the prison of her dress, his paintbrushes forgotten.

"Boy." The prince calls my name and my gaze intensifies on the canvas, resting idly on the easel, where Dolores looks back at me. Something akin to contentment hides inside her eyes. "I have told you to gaze upon your princess and admire her beauty and youth."

My gaze flickers to the prince, who stands behind her shivering body. His smile is malicious delight as he slips his thumbs into her undergarment and relieves her of the thin fabric, leaving her nude and exposed.

"Do not look at me, Two Three Six, adore your princess as you so love doing."

I bite my tongue as flames of hatred strike inside me. The new born flames spreads inside me, catching onto muscles and tendons, smouldering down to my very bones, scorching everything they touch till I can smell the stench of my body burning, the smell clinging to my nose hairs.

"Boy!" The prince's voice snaps my attention and my eyes refocus.

I inhale a breath, my charred throat dry and parched, and I cannot bear to look at her eyes, to find despair as deep as mine. Instead, I begin once more at the long column of her neck and count the slight protrusion of the ribs on her chest. I find three before my gaze falls on her breasts, milky and round adorned with dusky nipples that tighten in the cold room. I do not linger, but move on, following the curve of her waist and the arch of her hip bones, the collection of golden hair at the apex of her legs and then farther down till I reach her toes. Where my watery gaze remains locked.

"Do not pretend to be shy, boy, for I know how you delight in watching my princess."

I do not dare move. I have forgotten how to breathe. All I feel is the burn of hatred as it blazes through me, fierce and savage.

"You don't have to do this." Her broken whisper hacks through the thunder in my head.

"Oh, but I must, for how else would I capture your purity."

"Purity?" She whimpers and the prince coos.

"Do not cry, Princess, for crying is ugly and we are here for your beauty alone. Now kneel for me."

"Please…"

"Kneel." His icy tone leaves no room for argument. He places a hand on her shoulder and pushes lightly till she falls before him. "Good girl," he coos at her and my body shakes with fury so savage, I want to burst out of my own skin.

My grip tightens around my spear, my raw, angry skin stinging with pain and contempt. I think about the point of my spear piecing his perfect skin, the flood of angry blood that will spill from his body as it settles into the cavity of his heart where I so desperately want to bury it. And yet, I dare not move, or look, coward that I am, for I am afraid, not for myself, I do not fear death, it would be welcome relief, but for Dolores and what will become of her. I know the monster before me, but if I am gone, how can I protect her from the next one that takes his place.

"Boy." He calls my name and my gaze intensifies on the floor by her knees. I do not dare look up. I feel like a thief, stealing her secrets. "I have told you to gaze upon your princess and admire her beauty and youth."

I find her face, ashen and pale and marred in despair. Her eyes unfocused, like she's left the shell of her body and has escaped elsewhere. I wish to do the same.

He turns to the master. "She is ready."

The master nods and tilts his head. "She would be prettier still if her knees were not so tightly clenched together."

The prince slaps his thigh and shakes his head. "But of course, what better way to capture her inner beauty?"

Dolores doesn't need to be told, she squares her shoulders and stiffens her back. She spreads her knees apart till her buttocks rest on her feet and she is exposed. She does not spare any of us a look before her eyes glaze over once more and Dolores disappears.

The master nods in delighted appreciation before grabbing a paintbrush and striking out all but her face on his canvass.

The prince is back at my side. His sweat is acrid like his soul and he slithers a long finger along my jaw, coaxing my eyes to his.

"Ah, yes, I can see the anger inside you, *boy*, but you must remember to keep it buried. Do not think of acting upon it, for believe me, this"—he waves his hand around the room —"will be all but a fading joyous memory after what I shall put you through. Now, look upon your princess, take in her beauty and youth. Is she not magnificent?"

I stare at Dolores, my yes skipping over her three ribs over and over, watching her chest rise and fall in long, sad breaths that mimic my own.

Days stretch long and agonising as we meet in the bed chamber so the master can continue his work. A few strokes of paint before he needs to allow his canvas to dry. Each day I watch as the light fades more and more from my love's eyes, and her smiles are few and tight. And each day I am soaked in shame and racked with remorse as my treacherous body aches for relief, and forbidden images smoulder inside me as I explode beneath the streaming water, whispering her name.

The canvas is complete and the prince shakes the master's hand, clasping it in both of his. He invites Dolores to come and admire his handiwork. She sits on the floor lifeless and still and does not rise, nor look, nor acknowledge the prince's demand.

She is beautiful in her endless enduring strength and perseverance. The weeks have not shed from her pride and stubborn nature, nor have they filled her with hopelessness. Instead, as each day passed she has fortified herself with determination and hatred that burned as viciously and hot as mine, seemingly agitating the prince until his joy bled out and his impatience with the master bloomed like lotus.

"Princess," the prince calls out to her once more and this time she reluctantly meets his gaze, her eyes pointed, her jaw tight. She picks herself up stiffly from the floor and gathers a sheet around her, her movement precise and practices untouched by fear.

Her gaze flickers momentarily over the work, inhaling deeply, then exhaling the same long breath before thanking the master and requesting he take his leave if his work was done for she is tired.

"Do you not like the work, darling? Do you not want to marvel in the master's splendid work? For if you are unsatisfied, we can begin anew." The prince's finger strokes her jaw and lingers for a moment before he tucks away an errant hair behind her ear. Her eyes tighten with her fists around her sheet and she shakes her head. He waits for the red flush of her cheeks and for her eyes to fall away, for his thorn of humiliation to agitate her. But the princess does not yield to his twisted need. Instead, she steps closer to the canvas and studies it closely before turning back to her prince, whose nostrils flare like a pig's.

"The master has indeed created a masterpiece, but the making of it has rendered me tired."

The prince's jaw ticks and he snarls at the man, "Pick up your things and leave. Did you not hear my princess requires her beauty sleep?"

The master bows and collects his paints, stuffing them crudely into his leather bag before collecting his array of brushes and taking his leave.

Dolores glares at me from behind the prince and he follows her gaze. "Go!" He snarls at me as if speaking for her, but I remain still, my eyes locked on the cold marble of her eyes. She tips her chin and my heart trips before I take my leave.

The screams echo in the stone corridor and all I can do is allow them to soak through me as I watch the barred wooden doors. My hands ache as my grip keeps tightening on my spear and my muscles rage with tension. Time filters away in slow drips like a melting candle and I suffer through the harrowing sounds.

When the screams stop, the silence is even more threatening. The absence of sound claws at me like a deranged animal. The door creaks open and the woman hobbles out, her dress torn, her face streaked in tears, her bare back stained with the prince's cruelty. Her haunted eyes meet mine, but only for a brief moment before she turns away, silently creeping into the shadows to lick her wounds.

The door opens farther, the prince at its entrance nude and crazed, his chest an artistry painted in blood, his bed a rumpled wreck. On her own bed is Dolores, her grey eyes polished with unshed tears, horror etched into her face.

"We shall be ready momentarily," he announces as he makes his way to the washroom.

Without thought I rush into the room and fall at her feet. "Dolores," I whisper and her broken face tilts, till her eyes find mine and swirl back to life. "Did he hurt you?"

She shakes her head as I take her hands in mine, my metal armour keeping her warmth from me. "But if he finds you here he will hurt you."

"I don't care. I cannot bear to see him do this to you."

"It is not me he hurts."

I bite my tongue for fear of my thoughts spilling out.

"You must go. If he sees you here, he will take you from me, and that I cannot bear."

A single drop rolls down her cheek and slips into her mouth.

"Don't make me leave you with him."

"Tonight, beyond the gate. Wait for me." Her knuckles bleach around my armour that cannot feel her grip. "Please, return to your post. Tonight."

With a resigned nod, I withdraw and retake my post outside her chamber. *Tonight.* My body burns with her promise.

T he town is a foreign place to me now. It has grown and the wealth from the palace has leaked into the streets and the pockets of the once starved towns people. They thrive in trade and travel and, as I follow my princess on her horse, I glimpse an array of colourful tapestries, exotic foods, and unfamiliar contraptions. While I have been locked away in the palace, the world has flourished and expanded, growing a heartbeat that pulsed well beyond our borders and reaching over to new lands.

Those who do not stand behind stacked stalls trail behind us and crowd the streets. They cheer and throw flowers at my princess. They offer food and beg for their child to be kissed by her. Women reach out, grasping at her dress and running dirty hands over the cerulean fabric. The men seek to shake the hand of the man who will one day become their king. He offers them smiles and laughs with them as we make our way to the town hall.

The prince has kept his promise and Dolores—once recovered from this morning—has gathered her excitement. Her face is flushed with delight and her gaze wanders around the streets, consuming the enchanted, turbulent mess of the world beyond her high walls.

The parade ends at the hall where the prince and princess dismount and are followed by their admirers, who stream into the small building like a tempestuous lake. They babble and gush till the room is flooded with smell and noise and frenzied elation.

The prince stands and raises his hands. Silence falls across the room. He smiles and thanks them for their warm reception. They cheer and clap and burst into song. He is patient and charming and asks for silence once more. They obey, as they always will.

"Let me introduce you to the fairest girl in all the land, my betrothed, your princess Dolores." He holds out his hand and Dolores takes it. He tugs and she comes to stand beside him as the crowd erupts in a jubilant cheer. "This beautiful maiden who will one day rule by my side has expressed her love for you over and over again."

A red flush colours her face as the crowd cheers for her once more. "She has shared with me all her hopes and dreams she has for her people, for she loves you as her own. My precious Dolores has so much of herself to give."

His declaration sends a vicious tremble through me as his ugly words come back to haunt me *'He only has love for them. Love, it's his weakness, one I will never share.'*

"I have come today to show my beloved your beautiful town, for she is too sheltered inside her walls and can offer no real help behind them." The crowd nods and murmurs in agreement and he continues, "But also I have come to bequeath you all a gift."

A commotion in the back of the room draws the crowd's attention before they begin to part as two guards walk in carrying the gift. Dolores' eyes grow and her legs falter for a moment before she rights herself and her eyes beg for mine as a debilitating ache sears my chest.

The guards stand by their prince. Their armour black as his heart, glints in the intruding sun beams that push their way in, uninvited. He exchanges a few silent words and the guards begin the arduous task of setting the gift up on the wall. The crowd buzzes and churns around me, as Dolores grips the stone around her neck and squeezes her eyes shut.

Violent rage sweeps over me, and I search the crowd. I am outnumbered by the thousands, words, nor begging, nor violence will stop this, not even my death.

Dolores opens her eyes. Her hands drop away from the rock and she stands, tall and graceful, her strength magnificent as the prince unveils his gift.

"I give you my princess," he announces and his head whips around to gaze upon his final act.

The crowd stutters for a moment, taking in a collective breath as their eyes settle on the unveiled portrait of their nude princess. Women cover the eyes of their children and men's glares fester upon her body.

A silence deep as death settles across the crowded room till a thin voice shatters the silence, which crushes to earth like glass and splinters into a million pieces.

"Whore."

"Hag."

"Wench."

"Harlot."

Their calls trickle till they erupt, like a dormant volcano too long asleep and their heat scolds my princess as they gasp and laugh and jeer and leer. But even as a broken statue, cut down at the legs, she remains upright and beautiful, carved of courage and fortitude.

When we retreat back to the palace, the portrait remains behind guarded, to be forever gazed upon by the people she wanted to serve. The parade that follows us out of the town is no longer cheerful and delighted but lustful and deplorable as women cast their rotten fruit at my love and men tear at her dress, calling out to her, beseeching that she closes her legs around their waist and her lips around their bodies. I grab fistfuls of rage as I plow into them and shove them out of the way, silencing them.

She sits fixed on her horse, her eyes stone-cold and far away as we return to the safety of the castle, to which she is no longer desperate to escape.

The blaze colours the night sky in smoky yellow. It flickers and billows on the horizon. Shouts and screams rise up into the night. Leaning against the outer wall, I draw in long, shallow breaths and wait.

Time slithers slowly away, only my thoughts consume me like the bright hot flames of the blaze as it caught onto the old rotten wood of the town hall. How quickly the famished flames ate away at the building, igniting the night and outshining the stars. My thoughts continue to flare as angry and bright as the fire, months of contempt and desperation clawed away at me and until tonight I've had to wear my destruction on the inside. But as the town hall turns to ash, a wild, savage satisfaction pours inside me like water, soothing my scorched, blistered heart.

A shadow moves in the darkness and inches towards me, dragging me away from my thoughts. I settle farther against the wall, immersing myself in shadows when her breathless voice calls to me.

"Are you here?" she whispers and reaches blindly into the dark.

When she is close enough, I yank her into me and draw her in. She gasps then melts into me.

"Dolores," I whisper into her hair and breathe her in.

We hold on to one another, clinging on like saplings at

the edge of a cliff. I don't want to release her. "Were you followed?"

She shakes her head and keeps holding on to me as if afraid I might vanish if she releases me or perhaps that she may fall apart.

"Dolores, we don't have much time."

She nods and pulls slightly away, casting her gaze to the plumes of grey smoke that billow into the too bright night sky.

"What's happened?"

"There was a fire in the town hall."

Her eyes snap to mine. "You?"

"I could not allow him to—" But her hands are around me once more and she forces the air from my lungs as her grip tightens and she draws me closer still as if she wants to crawl inside me. Her body begins to quiver and shake and soon my shirt is wet from her tears as the dam of her emotions bursts and her strength slips away, making way for her vulnerability, pain, and fear, all pent-up inside her as she endured his cruel humiliation.

"Thank you, thank you," she chants against my chest and leaves small kisses on the fabric, each one sinking into my flesh and burying itself into my heart.

She cries, her jagged emotions spilling from her till my bones ache with her pain and my lungs fill with her grief and the thick air is too afraid to enter my body as I suck in breath after aching breath.

"I won't let him hurt you." I weave my fingers through her long locks and kiss her forehead. "He's already taken so much from you."

She sniffs and looks up at me, her tear-streaked face twisted and wistful. "He can never hurt me, not as long as you're safe."

"Dolores—"

"He can do what he will with my body, humiliate me,

force me to play his cruel games, but I have built a sanctuary around my heart, and that he can never touch. He can never take you away from me, for he doesn't know how much of you there is in everything I do." A melancholy smile tugs at her lips and her hand flutters up to her rock, chained around her neck.

"Princess..."

She arrests my words with the touch of her hand to my jaw, trailing the bristles that have sprouted on my face over the day.

"I wish you knew how I carry you with me everywhere I go." Her fingers slide over my neck and bury themselves in my hair. My body throbs at her touch and I look away from her ensnaring gaze, mine latching instead on her mouth. "You are a part of everything I do. Even the most trivial of tasks have a part of you under the surface of it."

At her whispered confession, I lose my veil of control and my lips collide with hers, spilling colour once again into my grey world. I silence the voices of my consciousness and allow myself to drown in Dolores, our kiss like the scorched town hall, possessive, urgent, desperate.

A scream echoes in the distance and I'm loathe to rip myself away from her lips. "Run away with me, Dolores. Let me take you away from here, from him."

Her hands fall away from me and her eyes squeeze shut beneath an avalanche of pain. She shakes her head. "I can't. He will hunt us down."

"We will outrun him."

"We will always be running."

"Running together." I reach for her hand and she yanks it out of my grasp.

"Restless, afraid. We will never be able to stop, we will never find solace."

"We will have solace with one another, in each other's arms."

"If he catches us, he will kill you, and I will endure a life-time of heartbreak." Her gaze softens on my face.

"I won't let it get to that."

"You have no say in his madness."

"Fine, return to the monster then." I abhor the untamed bitterness of my voice.

Her jaw wobbles as she reaches out to me. Her fingers feather over my skin before she cups my cheek and my brow furrows. Her eyes find mine, brimming with unshed tears, her beautiful face twisted with tortured emotion that mirrors my own.

I inhale and allow myself to sink into her touch, the palm of her hand soothing.

"I will find a way for us to be together."

I nod.

She pushes up and grazes my mouth with a whisper of a touch before she creeps back into the shadows and disappears beyond the wall, leaving me bathed with sweat and trembling with agitation.

I look into the darkening horizon, settling my thudding heart once more. The fire has died to a low simmer and I wonder if I too will end up a burned out skeleton of our love.

CHAPTER EIGHT

T he sky has never seemed so blue or perfect. We stand amid the flowers and petals simmering in the sweetly rising heat of springtime, but I cannot enjoy the sky or the garden or the moment. My stomach coils in vicious knots, my emotions jagged. I feel raw, as if there is no skin over my pain and the slightest breeze will make me bleed.

Dolores approaches. A laced veil held in place by a crown of daffodils hides her beautiful face. She glides over to where the prince stands and yet I feel her eyes transfixed on mine. It should make me delighted, but it only serves to make me sicker, nausea clawing its way up my throat and threatening to erupt from my bowels.

The prince stands tall, his dress suit as crisp as the day, not a hair out of place, an arrogant sneer smeared across his face as he watches his bride approach.

I cannot watch the bonding of their toxic union. Every promise spoken slits me open, leaching the strength from my body, straining my fractured heart. At the sealing of their coupling the crowd erupts in applause while my heart violently bisects. Two useless halves lie at my feet. I've wished for death before. But never more so than this moment where pain swells inside me in a poisonous flood.

I bite down the agony and endure the arduous task of watching my love being swallowed in the arms of another man, her lips consumed by the devil himself.

The king draws them each into his arms in turn and presents them to his guests, who leer and aster at my princess with distaste. "Today I welcome a son into my family, the man who will save my Dolores from the clutches of her cursed sleep and return her to us with nothing but a kiss." The cheerful crowd murmurs and falls silent as the king continues, "For tomorrow at the strike of midnight she will close her eyes and await her new husband's kiss."

The crowd cheers once more and I cannot distinguish jubilation from disdain as my own despair grows, sinking deep into my bones like toxic lead.

"Now enjoy yourselves, celebrate my daughter's birth and marriage, fill up on ale and food, for we are already saved."

The daylight dwindles to gloom as the celebrations mount. The festivities weave the crowd together and they ascend on the food and drink fluttering around the decadent tables like flies. They grow rowdy and jubilant while I, in turn, search for ways to salvage the remains of my heart.

I spot the old pedlar woman. She stands motionless in a crowd that flutters like flags in the wind, her black cloak shrouding her face in darkness and her piercing gaze fixed on me. My grip tightens on my spear as I tentatively approach her. She doesn't recoil or move as I make my approach. All the while she stands with her gaze locked on mine.

"Good evening," the woman greets me, her gaze dropping mine, instead fixing on the bride and groom locked in a slow dance that forces her body against his and his hands over her exposed back. I look away, scanning the crowd to see the leering men who tear away her gown with their eyes and the relieved maidens who had been touched by the hands of the prince thinking that with his marriage they will get a reprieve.

"You told me that you saved her, you told me I will too."

"I did, boy," she calls me affectionately and her tone baffles me.

I return my attention to her. "But you lied, you did not save her, nor have I."

"Will my curse not save her from the monster that holds her so boldly in his arms?"

My jaw ticks and my teeth grind and I concede. "It has not saved her from mystery or his cruelty."

"His cruelty is deep and dark as a well, endless in its depth, with no substance or life only murkiness and blackness, such is the expanse of his soul and should she remain awake past this day, he will unleash his true beast onto your princess."

My heart trips at her words. Your princess, she called her. As if she knows she belongs to me.

"I cannot rescue her from him."

A melancholy shadow passes over her eyes as she looks at Dolores. Her white dress sweeping over the green grass and her long, loose hair hung down like summer twilight. "You will, boy."

I follow her gaze. Finding my princess in another man's arms, her head tucked into his chest as his fingers dance on her skin and his face beams with malice. "How?" I ask, turning back to the hag who's vanished into the night.

My gaze swings across the crowd, searching for the hooded figure, knowing she will not be found.

I suffer through their dance and whispered words and stolen smiles and secret touches. Till night crawls in like a fanged monster and I am relieved. I escape, leaving my innards spilled on the dance floor to be trampled on by the prince.

The witch's words follow me like a shadow as I run like a coward and discard my armour, a farce, a shell that keeps me a prisoner. Hurt flares inside me, pricking my skin as I run. I squeeze my large frame through the palace gates and flee along the wall, my lungs fighting for air and my body screaming for relief. Pain stabs me from every direction till I collapse under the burden.

I lie on the cold earth, my arduous breath stinging my lungs as I stare into the starless night. The crescent moon peeks out from beneath the clouds, waiting to kiss my Dolores good night.

The snap of a twig drags me from my thoughts and back into the pain. I remain still as I search the darkness. When I see her my heart sparks to life as if a thousand fireflies take flight inside me. I lurch up and run to her.

"What are you doing here?"

"I want to be here with you."

"But it is your wedding night."

Her eyes fall away, brimming with tears. "It is also my birthday."

We both look up at the crescent moon. Dolores has indeed come of age.

"You must go to him."

"No, I want to be with you."

"Dolores."

Her gaze lifts slowly up to mine. "Tell me that you want me to leave. Ask me to go and be with him and I will."

I stare at my princess. The flower crown has been discarded and her hair flows like golden rivers over her shoulders, her white dress muddied at the hem and her eyes full of hunger that matches my own.

I shake my head.

"Then look at me, be with me."

"Dolores…"

"Gift me this one thing before I belong to him for eternity."

She's so close I can smell her flowery scent. It coils around me like thorny vines, tugging at my resolve. My mind is full of heat and sin and a clawing hunger that has nothing to do with my desires but everything with the way I feel about her.

"What you are asking for is forbidden, punishable by death."

"I'd rather die knowing I've had you in my arms for a single night, tasted your lips, and delighted in your body, than live forever never having had you."

"Dolores." I seal the distance between us and set my forehead to hers, our breath hot and fast, steep the air between us. I was hers and she was mine and for the first time I allowed myself to clutch at our unspoken bond.

I stand as if locked in stone, waiting. Slowly then, as if it was the first time, Dolores balances on her tiptoes and brings her mouth to mine, sweet and delicate and soft. She smells like earth and flowers and I allow myself to indulge in the softness of her chest that brushed against my hard one.

She falls away and her eyes latch onto mine. "I love you," she whispers and the words liquefy my insides.

My hand slithers into her hair and I bring her mouth to mine. My tongue passes the seam of her lips and our kiss is fervent and desperate as eighteen years of pent-up feelings spill from us. The more I taste her, the more of her I want and though I know what we are doing is wrong, I can no longer contain my feelings. Having Dolores for a single night will feed my starving heart till my last day.

I pull away from her mouth only to kiss her cheeks, her jaw, her neck. She drops her head back, allowing me access to her soft, beautiful skin, and I sample her flesh, memorising each salty note and fruity tinge, each decadent flavour that is Dolores. My hand reaches for the bow at the back of her dress and I tug gently. The fabric loosens and slumps over her shoulders.

Slipping my hands under the straps, I slide them over her shoulders and the dress pools at her feet. Dolores reaches for my shirt and rips it from my body and when I draw her into me, her flesh kisses mine, heat against heat, heart against heart. Freedom and terror grips me all at once as my fingers graze her nakedness and weave into her hair, and my mouth claims hers as mine.

My hands stroke her body and find her breast. We both gasp at the feel of my fingers brushing against her dusky nipple, which hardens and tightens beneath my touch. I am a lost explorer and her body is a map for me to discover and learn.

I set my discarded shirt on the red earth at our feet and lay my princess onto it. She gazes at me from below—her hair tossed and wild, her naked torso, her beauty fervent as the fiery moon. I blanket her with my body and her mouth is mine again, then her jaw and neck and when I taste her breast I want to shed tears of happiness and ruin.

Dolores is the banquet I have denied my starving heart. Every mouthful fills me, all her flavours unique and new and mine. I devour her as only a starved man knows how to feast, fast and slow, savouring and devouring, all my senses overwhelmed, every nerve awake.

I remove the last of her boundaries and inhale her intake of breath as I take in her nudity that she gives to me freely and willingly, not with force but with desire, and want. Her need spills into me, rippling through my skin and into my very bones.

I ravage my princess, making her mine with each kiss and lick and pass of my tongue over her curves, delighting in her hushed moans and needy gasps.

When my body can no longer take the strain, I pull away my garments and watch as her eyes rake over my nudity, appreciative and fearful, anticipating and hesitant, till her eyes sneak up to mine, her cheeks flushed in pink.

I lay myself above her, feeling the hot dew of her thighs as it screams for me.

My eyes latch onto hers. The marble churns and rolls like stone waves in a thunderous sea. "I won't hurt you."

"I know," she whispers over my mouth, her hot breath fanning my lips, which catch hers as I enter her.

A soft cry bleeds from her lush lips and I know even as I sink deeper into her warmth that this marks the beginning of my inevitable heartbreak and yet, I do not care. Her body beneath mine has erased all but us. All but the sweet sounds she makes as I move inside her, all but the quiver of her breasts as I thrust, all but the feel of her nails embedding themselves into my back, all but our bodies and breaths and skin, aching and taking what has been denied to us for so long.

In Dolores I find solace, safety, love. It brings me back to life, revives all that was taken from us and restores all that was shattered. Her body heals as much as her laughter or words ever did, and as I move inside her, faster and needier, I begin to break all over again.

A sheen of sweat wraps her beautiful face and her hooded eyes seek mine. I bury myself inside her, needing so much more than I can ever take, than I ever deserve. Our bodies slam into one another, breaking and reforming into something new, beautiful and devastating all at once. Our love is a beautiful wreck and wrapped in a twist of rotten silk.

My body shakes and quivers and for an instant the world vanishes and all I feel is pain and love and relief and anger and pleasure all blended into a singular word, "Dolores." I groan as my body empties itself into her and my mouth clamps around hers, seeking comfort.

When my breath returns, I remain above her, flesh to flesh, heart to heart, seeking only her heat and her eyes. "Did I hurt you, sweet princess?"

"A little." Her cheeks flush red. "But it was a good hurt." She seals her words with a gentle kiss. Her assurance alleviates the rock that threatened to settle in my heart.

I roll away from my princess and draw her into me, enjoying the feel of her skin against mine. "I love you," she whispers. Her hot breath sears my chest, and in that moment I fall, not in love, for I am already infatuated with my princess, but knowing she has used more than her body, but her heart and her mind, and our hope to love me. I fall.

I kiss the top of her head, breathing in new scents, hers mingling with mine, and my heart throbs with happiness. She peels her head from my chest and rests on her elbow. Her fingers draw circles on my chest.

"Tomorrow—" she begins and I set a finger on her lips and shake my head.

"I do not want to live in 'tomorrow', just in this moment with you."

"But—"

I swallow her words with a kiss. "Tomorrow all this didn't exist. Today I want to wallow in you, sate myself in you, embed myself into your very being so that in your sleep you remember only me."

Her fingers slide over my cheek before raking through my hair as she pulls my mouth to hers and gives herself to me again and again until our bodies are spent, drenched in sweat and coated in fine red dust. Our breaths belong only to each other.

I braid together these memories of her I have collected under the stars. The smell that drifts from the apex of her legs, the sounds she makes when I move inside her, the shape of her face as it changes and twists when her pleasure trembles beneath me.

Light blue tendrils drift across the sky, nudging away the darkness. I hold Dolores in my arms, her body warm and inviting, her heart beating in unison with mine.

Mine.

I'm loath to release my love and yet I do. I find her dress, no longer white, and help glide the fabric back over her body. I find my own garments and dress, feeling the weight of her gaze upon my body.

"You must go, Princess," I whisper, holding myself back, as if a glass barrier lives between us.

She nods. Her words would be nothing but arrows aimed at my heart. "I love you."

Her words bring me to my knees as she turns and runs into the fading shadows and to the arms of the monster who waits inside them.

My armour feels heavier as it clamps around my body like a metal coffin, suffocating me till all I hear is the dull pounding of a broken heart echoing around the tin.

The stone chamber echoes with my heavy steps where I find Dolores. She has been bathed and cleaned, her perfect skin lathered in creams, her nightgown white and crisp and her smile radiant. It glows through the darkness that's about to take her.

Her father kisses her forehead and whispers into her ear. She reaches for him and they embrace. She wipes her mother's tear-streaked face and kisses her gently before comforting her. The prince stands to the side, proud and tall like a parading peacock, but he does not approach her, nor speak. He awaits his turn. Where he can have her all to himself.

I inhale, drawing strength from fresh memories and Dolores' eyes sneak up to mine, locked together. Something potent passes between us and radiates in the room, entwining our souls and shivering with an unspoken truth. It's as if the rest of the room feels it too, for they all look up as if searching for something. Only the prince's gaze finds our connection and the eerie smile that presses his lips together sends a series of shivers along my spine.

She lies on the stone bed clad with flowers and perfume and her eyelids flutter. Heaviness drags her down until they fall shut. Her breathing eases till a gentle sigh that descends like billowing silk escapes her lips. The breath settles around the room, drifting towards the earth where it shall remain forever.

The colour drains from her skin, till she looks like living marble, perfect and cold yet warm to the touch, alive within her cocoon of stone.

When the eerie silence fills the room and my princess lies lifeless and unmoving like a statue, my heart constricts, my bones ache, and my lungs fill with impossible grief. Inhaling a few shuddering breaths, I whisper my short farewell.

Her captive audience remains staring. Time ticks by and she sleeps, unmoving. They know it will be a brief sleep, that her prince will lay his lips upon hers and she shall wake, and yet as if a worm of doubt has started nibbling on their certainty, they dwell, they are fearful, unsure. They question his love, they question his ability, they already miss their daughter.

They file out of the room in hopeful silence, all casting their eyes to the prince who carries their hope. When they have gone, I remain, bound to watch over my princess and keep my promise to her.

The prince approaches Dolores. His fingers slide over her cheek and trace the line of her jaw. "Still warm," he says almost to himself before he swivels around to face me. "You are relieved of your duty, Two Three Six."

I remain still, unmoving, my gaze locked on my beloved's lips, white and polished like marble.

"Ah, a true *friend*, till the very end, you do like to watch my princess, don't you, *boy*? Would you like to watch me touch her? Kiss her? Violate her? You know what she told me to do to her, don't you, *boy*? You know what she really wants?" He leers and licks his lips like a man about to feast. Demented anticipation floats across his crazed eyes.

I do not move. I cannot entertain the notion of his words. Not while she sleeps, not while she lies so helplessly in this chamber, deprived of life and light where only hatred can breed.

"As you wish, *boy*," he sneers. He turns to two guards who have stood silently by his side. "Make sure he watches."

If hatred were visible, the air would have been scarlet. I grip my spear in readiness and eye the two approaching men. Like me, they are clad in armour, but whereas my steel shines, theirs is black and dull as their master's heart.

"Fighting will only make it worse... for her," he says while gently brushing the long locks of golden hair out of her face.

I wince at his words as they split me down the middle. My body protests the onset of my defeat as my grip tightens. The men rush at me and I pounce, ready to meet their assault, when a sudden movement has me jerking my head back. But it's too late. Starburst explodes behind my eyes as my knees buckle and I fall to the ground. I taste a familiar copper tang in my mouth and wait for the room to stop spinning.

They strip me of my helmet and kick away my weapon. Heavy arms hold me in place, still I fight, trying to escape, to reach my princess, but to no avail. One of the trio produces a long, sharp knife that he leisurely slides along my throat in a cold warning. I still, the fight seeping away from me.

"You were warned, *boy*. Now witness the reward I take for your efforts." He licks his lips and his eyes dart over the sleeping beauty on the pedestal. "Do not cover your eyes, boy, for should you avert your gaze, I will punish her more." He awaits until my gaze follows him around the room and turns to my princess.

The prince retrieves a long blade. It glints in the dim light with dark ferocity before he slips it between her breasts and lets it rip away at the fabric. The threadbare nightgown melts away to the hem, lying open like broken wings hanging loosely over the stone bed that carries her lifeless body.

He gazes upon her naked body, all her forbidden curves and hidden crevices, a feast for his greedy eyes, before placing the blade to her shoulder, and ever so gently digging into her skin until it breaks and blood oozes from the wound like a red river. I moan and wince at her silent pain and regret the sound as it paints a demented smile on the face of the prince. Discarding his blade, it rings as it hits the marble floor. He dips his finger into the fresh wound and paints Dolores' lips till they are as red as a freshly picked apple.

He delights in his handiwork for a brief moment before his tongue, like a serpent's, begins to taste her body. Every inch of pale skin glistening with his trail. At her breasts he sucks on one nipple, then the other before he bites firmly into the flesh, marking her as his. The only mercy I have is that she sleeps. He slips down her body, his hands and mouth rough and brutal. He does not caress, but pierce and scratch. He doesn't kiss but bite and suck her skin till it screams with fresh bruises.

Tears bite at my eyes as he reaches the apex of her legs, covered by curly dark yellow hair. He pushes her legs apart and places his thumb over her pubis where he begins to rub and circle with maddening gentleness. My princess makes no sound, yet I hear her moans as they echo inside me. When his hands glisten, he pulls away and licks each one in turn, groaning as he does so, then stands and removes his garments, his erection hard and swollen, and he strokes himself admiring his handiwork.

"Your princess is a delicious treat," he lets me know as he mounts the bed on which she rests and parts her legs, pinching and scratching her inner thighs as he does so. He gathers her in his left hand and grips a nipple with the other, pinching mercilessly as he thrusts himself brutally inside her. His sigh is a long, agonizing taunt that clogs my throat with an onslaught of emotion.

He is a beast, thrust upon her, and she's nothing but a helpless bird, and his beast seeks to crush her bones and taint her skin so that no other could have her.

Only the clashing of skin on skin and the ragged sound of his breathing permeates the air. I can no longer hear my heartbeat that drummed so fiercely in my chest moments ago, for it lies lifeless and dead at my feet.

"Stop! No!"

The room freezes around me and too late I have realised my mistake.

"He speaks." The prince laughs. Her mouth falls open as he thrusts into her, but he does not seek comfort there, he does not kiss her red lips but instead, dips his fingers into the cavity and when he pulls them away, he stills and finds my eyes, his, demented pools of madness.

He climbs off my princess. Her thighs glisten with moisture, but he has not finished with her. Walking to the end of the bed, he pulls her shoulders so that her head drops slightly off the edge of the bed and her mouth falls open. The tip of his phallus kisses her red lips.

"No!"

"Your princess will choke on your lies." The prince laughs. The tip penetrates her mouth and he spears it with a violent thrust.

A burst of heat moves through my chest as the glass cage

I'd built around my heart shatters the shards tearing at my insides.

The prince delights as he watches me break before his eyes, violating her mouth, destroying her innocence like ice cracking stone.

He plunges in and out of her mouth, till his body shakes and his face contorts like a flower shrinking in the harsh sun. He empties himself onto her motionless face, smeared in blood and unmoving.

When he regains himself, he kisses her gently on the forehead before pressing his mouth to her ear. "Your curse is a delight indeed." He smiles at her bare body, bloodied and bruised.

He gathers his clothes and sets about dressing. He is casual and slow in his movement as if time is not an enemy that chases us to our grave. When he is done, he turns his attention back onto me. "Clean her, for I will return tomorrow, there's much work still to be done."

A shaky breath rattles out of me when he steps out of the room and I am released. I rush to my princess, whose body has been left discarded and desecrated upon her false altar. I set her back onto the bed as gently as one would carry a wounded animal. Her hair falls about her like a stained sun.

I caress her bloodied face, streaked with her own blood like a soldier after battle. She does not move, not murmur, nor does the pallor of her face change. She sleeps blissfully, unaware of the way in which her body was polluted. I wish to be blind, but even as I close my eyes I cannot unsee the horrors he has inflicted on my beloved, the way her body is nothing but a plaything to be wrecked and abused by a spoiled child.

When the guard brings the washcloth and water, he remains, his eyes not on me but on the marked body of the princess.

Wringing out the washcloth, I begin at her mouth,

washing away the blood and fluid, dragging it slowly across her skin, taking great care to erase any traces left by his hand. Pink water slithers between my fingers as I drain the cloth. Goosebumps bloom on her skin as I take my time with her, brushing over every inch of her once delicate skin, now bruised and marred, marked and destroyed by a monster.

The cloth washes away the smell of blood and sex and leaves behind a hint of spice and lemongrass. She does not smell like my princess. I do not hear my own strangled moans as they rip from my lips when I touch her damaged body. When I am done, I set aside the bucket and reach for her tattered nightgown. I pull at the frayed gown, but like my heart the seam no longer comes together. I set the cloth as best as I can to preserve what is left of her innocence before I stroke my fingers through her hair. The long, tangled curls catch and fall apart between my fingers as I brush the strands.

"I'm sorry," I whisper into her ear, as a deluge of cold pain threatens to bury me, but I cannot tamp the anger that burns inside, the failure that creeps around me like briar and slashes at my skin. I tried to stop loving her. I tried to save her, but all I ever did was fail her.

The slow, eerie clap echoes around the room and I slash my head around my shoulder to see the prince smirking at me. His eyes are dark and hollow and hold a stark promise that hides in plain sight.

Before I can move, arms hold me and the prince approaches, laughing, a low rumble that thunders in the cold room.

"Thank you, *boy*."

The muscles in my jaw jump as he rounds her body, pulling away the fabric and examining her wounds, delighting in the trophies he left on her.

"What a thorough job indeed." He runs a finger along her naked leg. "I do hope you enjoyed the last memory of your princess for now my guards will escort you beyond the wall. You may never return, never set foot in this palace again. She is mine now, and so she will remain."

"No!" I struggle against my captives, but he seems unperturbed by my resistance and reluctance to accept his threats.

"Ah, the liar dares open his mouth once more. I should cut out your tongue for your insolence, though taking her mouth was a greater pleasure." He bites his lower lip, sucking it into his mouth as if reliving the sensation.

Heat rises in my chest and anger claws its way to the surface, scratching at my skin. I bare my teeth and a pained, savage growl rips from me as I struggle and seek to lunge at him.

He stops mid stride, clucking his tongue. His eyes flash with dark intentions, before he smiles. A calm serene look spreads across his face and spikes a shiver of fear that races through me like a glacier. "Keep your tongue, *boy*, but should you ever return, *she* will pay with pounds of flesh and not mere playful lacerations."

I search his eyes only to find the truth in his threat. He pulls out his blade once more and slithers it gently over her skin then, with a flick of his wrist, slices away at her body, removing an inch of flesh.

"No!" I struggle with my captives, as a thin stream of blood leaks from her fresh wound, pooling beside her. Starburst flashes behind my eyes and the world tilts on its axis. Gravity ceases to exist and all light dies out in an instant.

It's the shivering that stirs me awake, the trembling of my body seeking to keep itself warm. I bolt upright, my head swinging as I search for my Dolores, but I am no longer in the room, no longer in the palace. I scramble to my feet and search the horizon in the descending darkness. There is naught around me but green swaying seas of grass that dance in unison under the chilly wind. It whips the blades back and forth and pierces my naked skin.

I run, the direction does not matter as long as it brings me closer to Dolores, for the witch promised I would rescue her. Just as she has, and yet the prince's promise shudders inside me like icicles. I stop, my head whipping with the wind, seeking direction. I am lost, and my heart is lost, and my Dolores is lost.

I fall to the ground, allowing my body to feel the exhaustion of the day. The pit of my stomach aches as I water the grass with my pain.

CHAPTER NINE

The ocean is bleak and endless, unlike the vast warm blue Dolores described to me once. In my dreams, our fingers sifted through the sand and the waves kissed our toes. Yet, these hostiles, rolling waves nip at my feet as I stare into another horizon.

I have been wandering. Only the moon and stars guiding my path as I search for my princess. This land is foreign and cold, hostile in ways that hurt only my aching body. Yet I am not deterred, not by the biting chill or burning sands, nor by the familiar hunger that has clawed its way back to me after so long.

I turn away from the water and trudge in a new direction, towards another horizon.

My raw feet sink into the golden sands and scream at me, they beg me to stop, and yet my heart protests the notion. My tongue runs over chapped lips and my shoulders ache while my arm shelters my face against the fierce wind. Dust coats my skin, invading every crevice and hollow. My muscles burn as I fight the harsh sun and climb yet another dune just to find another empty horizon.

I turn my back to the wind and the sun and let their laughter die at my back as I keep searching.

I lean against the bark, letting the shade cool my heated skin. I have wadded through this brush and briar, through the maze of trunks and pitch-dark of the canopy just to end at the edge of the world. A sheer drop opens before me, a splendid vista of endless greens and blues, and yet the horizon mocks me, for once again it is empty.

Thorns slice my feet and catch my ragged clothes as I descend in search of a new horizon.

The town looks almost familiar. The narrow streets are full of haggard-faced peddlers that carry grief on their backs like boulders. But this town is not as I remember it. The colourful market and exuberant foods are gone. Poverty and hunger have returned to haunt them as they huddle in corners and fill their stomach with smells.

It is the familiar aroma that has me snapping my neck to the west. There, amongst overgrown bramble and thorny burr lies the castle. An overgrown monstrosity that has held my princess in its prison.

I step closer, slowly, my heart in my throat. The first beat takes me almost by surprise. It has been lying dormant for so long I did not recognise the pulse when it came alive. I stare at the horizon that has so long avoided me. Tears spring to my eyes, and relief washes over me in agonising waves of joy and sorrow. My knees kiss the cobblestones. They dig and scrape my wounded skin and tears streak down my cheeks in endless rivulets for, at last, my search is over.

I do not know how long I expel my demons into the pavement, but when I get up, a gentle calm sets itself upon me and I know I must ready myself.

The tavern is dim and deplorable as the rest of the town and the serving wench greets me with a toothless smile that doesn't touch her haunted eyes. She sets ale and hard bread before me.

"What has happened here?" I ask her before she turns away.

She looks at the blackened walls as if searching for ears in the shadows. "We have all been cursed," she whispers.

"Cursed?"

She sighs, resigned, and lowers herself to me so that her face is lined with mine. "Many years ago the people took on a new prince, they worshipped him and loved him at the expense of his princess. When he shamed her before them, they leered at her instead of ousting him." She looks over her shoulder like perhaps she may be looking for forgiveness. When none comes, she continues, "The princess fell asleep, and a darkness set over the town. The rains haven't returned and the green fields turned yellow and died away, the winters lasted longer and the traders who feared the curse might be contagious stopped coming. Ports were closed and towns shut their gates to us and slowly we began to suffocate on our own sins."

My heart slams in my chest as I listen to her story. "What of the king?"

The woman shakes her head and her shoulders drop heavily. She looks older than she should, life tugging at her face and pulling it down. "The king is dead."

"Dead?"

"Some say it was the shame that killed him. It blackened

his soul to realise he gave his daughter to a devil that had no intent on saving her. Others say it was despair that took him."

"The queen?"

"Joined her husband in the grave, unable to remain abandoned in her own home."

"What of the princess?" My heart trembles with the question.

The woman's lips purse together. "Whispers from the castle say that she has been cast into stone, that she will never wake. She has doomed us all."

The woman turns to leave, and I grab at her arms in desperation. "There was a woman once, a baker. She lived inside the castle walls. Agatha."

The woman shakes her head. "All inside are cursed."

She leaves me to the stale bread that lodges in my throat as I swallow down her words.

I stare out of the murky window at the castle that lies beyond. I am so close to her and yet I cannot seem to close the distance between us. Fear and uncertainty wiggle beneath my skin like worms.

Since her youth, she has shown such irrational affection towards me that I had always expected it to vanish as abruptly as it has started. Things fall apart as is their nature.

Love is not sturdy but a delicate thing that needs to be nourished and protected. It is not robust, it is not unyielding, it can crumble under a few harsh words or be tossed away with a handful of careless actions. It isn't steadfast or permanent. Dolores' love for me seemed built on such flimsy a premise that I assumed it would come apart the moment I woke her. How can love based on fear and despair survive? It was impossible. And yet my heart yearned for it to be true, and I could not deny my own desires, my own burning love that has engulfed me since the day of her birth.

I have allowed time to trickle by. Most days are dull and grey, full of remorse, and when I visit my memories, it is like visiting a graveyard full of old versions of myself. They come out to haunt and taunt me. The searing pain that has accompanied me with each sunrise has eased to a throbbing pain, an aching reminder of my failure and the prince's promise.

I drank of course, to fill the bottomless chasm in my soul, and when that wasn't enough, I learned to quench my thirst with trouble. My fists are calloused and war torn as I leave pieces of my flesh on the faces of my enemies. I have grown stronger, and crueller, as I emptied my ruined heart.

Yet today I have woken up in knots. My body quakes like a drenched puppy and her voice calls to me, vibrating through my bones as if our souls are still irrevocably tethered. I sit on the edge of my bed as resolve trickles inside me like sand. I cannot bear another sunset without her, another day, not knowing what has become of my love. The palace, now overgrown and threatening collapse, has greyed and aged in the same way that I have.

The cold water flows along my wrinkles and drops down my chin. The sun and elements have beaten down on me, my once young supple skin now coarse and calloused, my jet-black hair infused with greys and whites. As I gaze at the castle, I wonder if she will recognise the man she once knew.

I dress, feeling lighter than I have in many moons. A contentious smile tugs at my lips. They have forgotten how to smile without her. I do not look back when I walk out of the door of the place that has kept me warm and dry and housed my suffering in silence. I do not carry anything with me but hope and tremendous joy as I make my way towards the palace, where my beloved awaits.

My aching feet drag along the red sand, which swallows the blood I have fed it. The shadows embrace me as I scamper along the familiar walls, now held up by vines and creepers that have pushed their way through the gnarled cracks. I creep along the wall till I arrive at the old gate, just to find it has further collapsed without repair. My hearts stammers in my chest as I peek into the devil's den.

Only the dark greets me.

I push my way through the crack and skittle along the walls. Much looks the same and yet it has somehow changed, touched by time and the elements. I do not wallow. I wait, and when I see him, I strike hard and fast. The guard collapses like a tin man at my feet. I drag away his body and seize his armour as my own.

The steel shell smells of death and cruelty, but my footsteps remain alight as I steal into the castle, navigating the maze of walls and halls to the place my heart aches to be. I stand at the door and listen. The silence tries to hide the savagery hidden inside the room, and yet the prince's every motion permeates through me like waves.

I slide into the room and into the darkness. In my absence I have perfected the art of being overlooked, and now as the prince is deep inside my Dolores, I am as unnoticed as the long cobweb that hangs precariously from the ceiling above. The room is vacant save the three of us. His groans and murmurs bounce off the walls that have witnessed his malice and anger.

I strip away the armour silently, as I watch his body slam into hers, a belt whipping mercilessly at her torso. Blacking the flesh. The old flame of anger sparks into life as I watch him mutilate my love. Fury burns inside my veins, setting me alight, a ferocious, unstoppable blaze that will scorch anything in its way, deadly and unstoppable.

When I am free of my steel prison, I relieve my blade from my belt and creep towards the centre of the room. I lunge at the prince and rip him away from my beloved. He squeals with surprise, sounding like the pig he is. I drag him across the floor and bring my blade down upon him. His hands rush to the wound, but I bring my blade down a second time, ripping flesh and severing skin until his ivory skin turns red, like the roses in the winter garden.

"*Prince* Aamon, at last I have returned to rescue my princess."

His eyes search my face. His eyebrows gather in a sharp V before his eyes grow wide and recognition sets in. Like with all of us, his youth has been stolen by time, which has blunted his features yet sharpened his cruelty. He tries to speak, but only a wet gurgle escapes him as life seeps away from his body in a bloodied flood.

I smile then, fulfilled in the notion he knows I am the bringer of his death. He tries to reach up, but I push his hand away easily. "You have forced me to watch many deplorable things, but watching your death will bring me the greatest pleasure, comparable only to your wedding night, when I enjoyed taking my beloved's innocence."

He gags in my arms as if the words he seeks to say choke him, and nothing has ever thrilled me as much as watching the dark light fade in his eyes as he struggles to gasp his last breath.

I leave him there, a corpse on the floor, and run to my princess where she lies on her stone casket. Her beautiful face hasn't aged, the skin hasn't gathered around the eyes from laughter and pain. Her body, though bruised and used, has remained as it was on the night of her eighteenth birthday, shapely and perfect in its curves.

My heart, which till this moment has felt as if it has forgotten how to beat, comes to life. The rhythm spikes in an out of tune rhythm. With my hands bloodied and heart in ruins, I kneel by her and kiss her cold lips till warmth seeps into them and she moans into my mouth, awake.

I wrench myself away from her lips, which respond to

mine, seeking and needy. My heart falters in my chest as her eyes flutter slowly open.

'I saved her, boy, and one day you will too.' The witch's voice swims inside my head as elation drowns me, for at last I have broken her cruel curse and fulfilled my destiny.

Dolores licks her wet lips and her eyes open and close as if the dim light pains her. She cranes her neck from side to side, her eyes squeezed shut as if she doesn't want to let go of a dream.

Her body wakes in slow motion, movements of ice melting away from flesh. The colour returns to her as if a painter adds strokes of colour to her flesh.

She moans as if her throat hurts and swallows. My lips ache for hers. I want to soothe her broken body. As the colour returns, so must the pain as her face twists in an agonised grimace. A low groan seeps from the seam of her lips.

"Dolores," I whisper her name and twirl my hands in the locks of her hair, no longer limp but lush and rich. It entwines between my fingers, the ends tickling my palm, which has craved her flesh for so many moons.

At my voice, her eyes barrel open and her gaze studies me. A weak hand lifts to my face and her palm cups my cheek. I hold it there, feeling her warmth.

"Are you real or am I still in my dreams?" Her voice is broken and hoarse. Her lids droop and close, her body still remembering how to wake.

"It's real. I'm here, I saved you."

It is as if my words send fire into her veins and the last of the ice melts and breaks away from her.

Her eyes fly open and her gaze dances over the room. It flutters over me and she recoils.

"Don't be afraid," I whisper, waiting for her to study me. To see me.

Her fingers flutter over the map of wrinkles now set on

my face, long crevices forged by worries and angst as I made my way back to her. She stares into my eyes, the long crow's feet that stretch around them like crumpled parchment, and rakes her fingers through my beard, thick and bushy streaked with white. She sees me not as who I was but as an old man, beaten and forlorn.

"Is it really you?" her broken voice asks again. Her melancholy notes strike a chord inside my heart.

I nod and smile at my beloved.

"What did you do?" Her voice trembles and her gaze roams around the room. Tears sting her eyes before they leak slowly onto her cheeks. Her tearful gaze lands on the slain prince that lies lifeless and bloodied on the floor.

She slips off her bed and staggers to the dead man on the floor, tears leaking from her eyes as she cradles him against her chest.

Confusion grips me as I kneel before her, watching in horror as she strokes his lifeless face, "My princess?"

She turns to me and our eyes collide, hers full of sadness. "What did you do?"

"I saved you."

"No." She shakes her head. "You've doomed me."

"My love?"

"In my dreams, we were together. I felt your warmth in the darkness. I felt comfort in my solitude, knowing you were watching over me. In that place we were together."

"We can be together still."

"Can't you see?" Her soft fingers reach over to me and trace the scar left there as a gift by her prince, painting me in his blood like a battle worn warrior. "I could never be with a man like you."

"A man like me?" My heart lurches inside my weakened chest.

Her eyes soften as she speaks, "A guard, a servant. You've doomed me to a life of servitude, if not with this cruel prince then another. My father will marry me off to the next in line." She shivers and runs a hand into his hair. "My prince agreed not to wake me. He promised to allow me to live inside my dreams where I could be with you for all eternity, in exchange for my body. You haven't freed me, my love, you've cursed me all over again."

"Your father is dead, as is the prince. We are free. We can run."

"My father—"

"Died a broken old man, drowning at his own despair, for he gave his only daughter to the devil himself." Her eyes fall away at the harsh sting of my words. My knuckles find her chin and I coax her head up till our eyes lock.

Her laugh is bitter and sorrowful, turning my heart cold, a heavy stone set in my chest. "You have murdered a prince and suggest to take away the princess. We will always be hunted. We will never know peace."

The truth of her words sheets my skin with a chill. "Dolores."

Her eyes swell with tears, which fall like stars down her beautiful face, the end of dreams.

"Do not cry, Princess, there is still so much life to live."

"Without you?"

I stroke her shoulder, thrilling in the touch of her skin. "I will always be here."

She shakes her head. "You must run. You can never look back." Her eyes flicker over to the dead man at her feet before they return to mine.

"I won't leave you again," I say and she steps into me, ripping the space between us.

"You never did."

Her lips are warm and soft and the kiss is slow and drugging like she wants to pull me back into her dreams. Chaos blooms in my chest as her nails drag along my scalp and her tongue tastes mine. When she breaks our kiss, emptiness grips me. My body aches for more of her.

"Dolores," her name is a breathless groan. Her kiss has shown me that her love was not feeble as I feared but powerful and unbreakable. Her love for me had not festered in her sleep but grew so big it spilled from her heart and filled not only the room but the entire palace.

"I want to see the moon," she says dreamily.

I search her face and look for the girl I once knew. Her endless hopefulness and joy that throbbed through her with every heartbeat, the one who so freely shared her love with the world, yet I find only a single weak flame she carries for me while the rest has been snuffed away.

I straighten my spine, searching for a well of strength I'm no longer sure I possess, nod, and take her hand in mine. We leave behind the stone chamber now a tomb, before I lead her to the tower and up the narrow winding stairs that held our secrets in our youth.

I use my shoulder to push open the door above us. Dust rains down as it flips open and the icy air rushes inside and sweeps across my face. Beside me Dolores gasps, then delights in the vanishing puff of heat that escapes her mouth in a cloud.

"Help me," she whispers. A flush sets in her young face and her eyes search the sky above us.

My knees groan as I kneel before her and lace my hands together, anticipating her touch. When she grips my shoulder, her foot lands on my hands and I push her up. A flurry of hair tickles my face and a satisfied sigh echoes down as Dolores pulls herself out of the opening and onto the roof. I stretch out my aching arms and pull myself up.

I watch my princess see the world again as if for the very first time. But this new world is not as she remembers. Bleak and dark as the prince, her land sits in ruins and despair.

In this place where we sat as children and shared our

dreams, all her dreams have come to die, all her hopes shattered and broken with a single kiss. Mine. The thought rips through me like loud thunder, bouncing around my bones and bringing me to my knees.

"What happened here?" She searches the dim horizon where green fields are now nothing but ashen earth and where life once flourished there is nothing but death and destruction.

"Sadness and darkness overtook them, and nothing can grow in the dark, nothing can grow without love and nourishment. They loved you and chose him and in that lay their demise."

"I have taken everything away." Her face forlorn and haunted spears my soul.

"No, beloved, these punishments were inflicted on them by their own actions."

Her downturned lips press together and her eyebrows gather in a sharp V over bleak, glistening eyes. "My birth has brought nothing but death and misery to all I love."

I take her hands in mine and bring them to my heart where I settle her palms over the beat. "Your birth has brought me nothing but joy."

Her lips tip up ever so slightly and she gifts me with a chaste kiss that tastes like hope.

"The moon looks beautiful tonight." The crescent smiles at my princess as she gazes at its light. The marble of her eyes swirls with its brightness. "In my dreams I learned you better than I knew my own thirsty heart, your sweet lips and strong arms. We were engulfed in happiness."

"Princess." My choked throat slick with emotion. My jaw wobbles as I watch her. She shivers in the freezing night air, her torn nightgown offering no protection from the elements. Her body peaks out beyond the tattered fabric and my body craves those dreams. "There is happiness to be had here."

"No." She shakes her head. "It will be too brief and too painful. You shouldn't have killed him."

"I couldn't endure one more sunrise without you, for while you've been sleeping, I have been searching for you."

Her face falls and she steps precariously closer to the edge, her feet resting on the rotten piece of timber I installed there after her near fall all those years ago.

"Save me," she says as tears fall recklessly down her cheeks.

"Dolores..."

"Take me back to my dreams, be with me forever, my love."

Her words like a blade, rip into my spine and slam in my chest. I know what she asks of me, and my dead heart bursts to life. I step towards my princess and cradle her in my arms. Her cold body warms my own and my heart burns against hers.

We step closer to the edge, the wood crumbling slowly beneath our feet, as my lips find hers. I capture her mouth in a kiss, languishing in her taste, the feel of her against me. The smell of earth and flowers permeates my senses as we fall.

The crescent moon smiles at us as we stare into each other's eyes, the world inching ever closer. Warmth encompasses me, as I fall for my love, with my love, and into her dreams where we can always be together, for at last I have saved her.

Sun bathes us in liquid gold seeping into our bones, tattooing her name forever onto my bones.

The pain is exquisite.

If you enjoyed this story, why not leave a review on Amazon and Goodreads to tell everyone how much you loved it?

ACKNOWLEDGMENTS

I would like to start by thanking you, the reader, so much for reading! If you enjoyed the story, please leave a review and recommend the book to any friend you think would love this story. You will have my eternal love and gratitude.

A massive thank you to Tracey Caldwell, your input and encouragement has been amazing.

To K, despite your *still* terrible taste in beverages, when you're not the worst, you're the best. Another book that wouldn't have made it to the shelf without you. You know how much your input, laughter and late nights mean to me. Thank you x.

ABOUT THE AUTHOR

Jane Wynters doesn't quite know how to answer the question of "where are you from?" She's moved from place to place like a snowflake on the wind always searching for a safe place to land. She loves meeting new people and exploring new places. She loves reading, writing and conjuring new worlds from her imagination. Coffee is at the top of her food pyramid and she is fluent in three languages, her favourite being sarcasm.

Want to know more about the author and keep in touch? Get snippets of upcoming books and have a bit of twisted fun?

Come join me in Wonderland...

ALSO BY J. A. WYNTERS

Standalones

Guarding Gabriel

Fractured

The Beverage Wars

Mai Tais and Goodbyes

Parts of Me Series

Spare Parts, Book 1

Fixed Parts, Book 2

Broken Parts, Book 3

Torn Apart, Book 4 (Preorder now available)

Picked Apart, Book 5 (Coming Soon)

The Fractured Fairytale Series

Beast

Wolf

Hunter (Preorder now available)

Dreamer